# DONUTHEART

# DONUTHEART

Sue Stauffacher

**Alfred A. Knopf**
New York

THIS IS A BORZOI BOOK PUBLISHED BY ALFRED A. KNOPF

Published in the United States by Alfred A. Knopf, an imprint of Random House Children's Books, a division of Random House, Inc., New York.

KNOPF, BORZOI BOOKS, and the colophon are registered trademarks of Random House, Inc.

www.randomhouse.com/kids

Educators and librarians, for a variety of teaching tools, visit us at
www.randomhouse.com/teachers

Grateful acknowledgment is made to Alfred A. Knopf, a division of Random House, Inc., and Harold Ober Associates Incorporated for permission to reprint "Poem" and an excerpt from "Passing Love" from *The Collected Poems of Langston Hughes* by Langston Hughes, copyright © 1994 by The Estate of Langston Hughes. Reprinted by permission of Alfred A. Knopf, a division of Random House, Inc., and Harold Ober Associates Incorporated.

*Library of Congress Cataloging-in-Publication Data*
Stauffacher, Sue.
Donutheart / by Sue Stauffacher — 1st ed.
   p.  cm.
SUMMARY: Usually preoccupied with his own concerns about hygiene and safety and with his crush on Glynnis, sixth grader Franklin Delano Donuthead finds that he is unaccountably worried about his mother's feelings and his friend Sarah's difficult home life.
ISBN-13: 978-0-375-83275-8 (trade) — ISBN-13: 978-0-375-93275-5 (lib. bdg.)
ISBN-10: 0-375-83275-0 (trade) — ISBN-10: 0-375-93275-5 (lib. bdg.)
[1. Interpersonal relations—Fiction. 2. Courage—Fiction. 3. Self-actualization (Psychology)—Fiction. 4. Ice skating—Fiction. 5. Middle schools—Fiction. 6. Schools—Fiction.] I. Title.
PZ7.S8055Don 2006
[Fic]—dc22
2005032553

Printed in the United States of America

October 2006

10 9 8 7 6 5 4 3 2 1

First Edition

For the Gilles boys—Roger, Max, and Walter—my treasures on earth

When you get to the end of your rope, tie a knot and hang on.

—Franklin Delano Roosevelt

# Fear of Flying

In the course of human events, it is sometimes necessary to reduce one's water intake to delay natural functioning. Using the boys' bathroom at Pelican View Middle School was to be avoided whenever possible. I will spare you the details of my first visit; it's enough to know that it involved me, Franklin Delano Donuthead, an industrial-sized roll of toilet paper, and an eighth grader's knowledge of ancient Egyptian mummification techniques.

The problem is, the adolescent body is 75 percent water. And what goes in must come out. Just not in the boys' bathroom. Note that I did not say "the boys' and girls' bathrooms." All you need is a peek through the open door to realize that girls can attend to their business behind closed doors. I am still working through my feelings about this. Who decided—and then proceeded to tell generations of architects—that boys need less privacy than girls? Who? Girls are always saying they want everything to be equal. Hello? The restroom facilities are not equal.

Principles such as equality are as important to me as they were to my namesake, Franklin Delano Roosevelt. "Rules," our late, great thirty-second president liked to say, "are not necessarily sacred. Principles are." So I maintain a strict code of conduct based on my interpretation of the principles set forth by President Roosevelt in the New Deal. These include:

Mental Improvement

Health Promotion

Risk Avoidance

The sad state of boys' bathroom facilities had not yet hit the national scene when FDR was in office. Understandably, he had to figure out the Depression and World War II first. Historians could also argue that FDR was more concerned with job security than risk avoidance. But I am living proof that times have changed, and the order of the principles needs to be shuffled around a bit for the new century.

So every time I stand outside the boys' bathroom, health promotion and risk avoidance start duking it out in my mind.

Health promotion: *Pee! You've got to!*

Risk avoidance: *Are you kidding? Protect your vitals!*

Health promotion: *Use the staff bathroom by the office.*

Risk avoidance: *What if Coach Dilemming's in there!?*

By the sixth week of sixth grade, my tendency to avoid risk was winning on a daily basis, and my lack of fluids was affecting my overall level of health so dramatically that I was forced to do what I try very hard not to.

And that is to interrupt the early-morning reverie of the chief statistician for the National Safety Department in Washington, D.C. Her name is Gloria Nelots, and I happen to know that at six-thirty a.m. she is at her desk at department headquarters, drinking a cup of very strong coffee with powdered cream and artificial sweetener and synchronizing her handheld to her computer's notebooking system.

Gloria: This better not be you, Franklin.

Me: Is that how you answer an agency line, Gloria? What if I were your boss?

Gloria: I have it on good authority that he is on the treadmill in the company gym at the moment. (*Long silence. Gloria is a bit grumpy in the morning.*)

Me: Gloria, have you ever heard of a condition called "paruresis"?

Gloria: I can't say I have, Franklin.

Me: Really? I'm shocked.

Gloria: Well, are you going to enlighten me, or will I be forced to return to enjoying the early-morning quiet, which is the very reason I come to work before the rest of the department?

Me: Happy to. Basically, it's a fear of urinating in public.

Gloria: Last I heard, that was illegal.

Me: I'm not talking about the alleys next to bars, Gloria. I'm talking about designated public places. I'm talking about bathrooms . . . public bathrooms . . . as in the presence of other . . . well, boys . . . eighth graders to be precise. Members of football teams.

Gloria: You're having trouble letting it fly at school? Is that what you called me at 6:37 a.m. eastern standard time to discuss?

Me: Yes!

Gloria: My advice is, turn on the faucet before you unzip. Works wonders.

Me: But—

Gloria: The call buttons are lighting up here, Franklin.

Me: I don't hear any ringing.

Gloria: Nevertheless. Busy, busy. Oh, I almost forgot. How is Sarah? Has she picked out a costume yet?

Me: I'm afraid we're having a little trouble in that department as well.

Gloria: Really? You'll have to fill me in on that later. I'm still good for the bill. Have Julia send me the receipt straightaway.

Me: The trouble is . . .

Gloria: Good-bye, Franklin.

Why Gloria and my mother are so wrapped up in Sarah Kervick's life is a complicated matter that I haven't yet been able to completely puzzle through. Sarah arrived in Pelican View eleven months ago, during our fifth and final year of elementary school. At that time, my mother helped her out with certain . . . difficulties. Sarah does not at present have a mother, so she relies on mine to consult with about hair, clothes, and her overriding passion—figure skating. Gloria has also taken an interest and helps pay for Sarah's training and other expenses. I cannot for the life of me figure out why these two women should exercise what little maternal instinct they have on Sarah Kervick when clearly I, too, am in need of a mother's loving care.

Especially now that I am in middle school.

But every time I turn around—Sarah Kervick! For example, out of the blue, my mother informed me that Sarah and I would be performing our community-service activities together. As part of Pelican View Panthers Civic Pride Week, which is always the first full week after Labor Day, each sixth grader must sign up for twenty hours of community service to be completed during the school year to show that we are doing our part to make the world a better place.

When I tried to protest, my mother said: "You have to find something to do together because my new schedule doesn't give me enough time to take you separate places. Need I remind you, Franklin, that it's a requirement? And Sarah has to meet all school requirements in order to skate."

So there we sat at the kitchen table, my mother and Sarah unwrapping Twinkies at a rapid rate and sprinkling sticky crumbs all over the list of volunteer options.

"This one looks like fun," my mother said. "We could all do this together. They need three volunteers to stamp hands at the Lions Club Charity Carnival for Kids."

I happen to know that my mother's boyfriend, Paul Bernard, belongs to the Lions Club. Honestly, it's like she has antennae for anything that will get her more face time with Paul.

"Sure," Sarah mumbled, her mouth full of Twinkie cream.

"I think not," I told them. "I just heard on the news it's going to be a banner flu season."

"So?"

At times, it was necessary to connect the dots for Sarah.

"All those germy little hands would put us at high risk for infection."

"All right, all right." My mother's finger traveled down the list.

"What about raking leaves for the elderly? You can't catch anything from leaves, can you?"

Sarah shrugged. She couldn't think of anything. Once again, it was up to me.

"Certain forms of mold can be very hazardous to your health. A pile of leaves is a veritable breeding ground for mold spores."

My mother gave me that look, the one where she raises both eyebrows half an inch. She returned to examining the list.

"Here's one: Search the Internet from your home computer for possible health threats. Then tell other people in agonizing detail about the many ways they can die."

"Very funny."

Sarah, who had just taken a big swallow of milk, managed to choke it down before bending over in her chair and cracking up at my expense.

"Or at that Lions Club thing," she said, "I can dip their hands in bleach before Franklin stamps them." This got my mother going.

Study after study has shown that a good sense of humor aids longevity, so I was willing to overlook the general gaiety at my expense. However, I did not understand *why* this was funny. Since I'd begun middle school, my risk factors had skyrocketed. Who could blame me for trying to stay safe during extracurricular activities?

You see, while there are many opportunities for mental improvement, health promotion and risk avoidance are very difficult to attain in the middle-school environment. Instead of one classroom and one teacher, I now have seven classrooms, seven teachers, and approximately 478 students to jostle past on any given school day. This last figure takes into account students in more than one class and students within range of my locker. Believe you me, 478 is a conservative estimate.

And that's just standing still. When I'm on the move, things get even more hazardous. We have a mere four minutes between the end of one class and the beginning of another. Due to a bizarre growth pattern, which I am charting for scientific purposes, I find it difficult to "make tracks" in the hallway. You see, one side of my body is longer than the other by almost half an inch. My left arm and leg are outpacing my right arm and leg, making balance, coordination, and participation in any gym or sports activities very difficult for me, though I have yet to convince anyone else of this belief, including Ms. Wolf, our gym teacher.

I do the best I can with what I've got, but on my very first day, I got tangled up in what I call "The Ponytail Express," a complicated relay of feminine persons darting back and forth across the hallway. I have observed that a girl with new information to convey has the right-of-way despite the general traffic pattern. Smacking up against unfamiliar girls who act as if *I'm* the one at fault is really quite stressful. And I haven't even mentioned the lunchroom, or the boys' locker room. *Or* any of the three boys' bathrooms.

As you can see, simply getting through the day intact had become my new challenge. And every time I thought things couldn't get worse . . . they did.

On Tuesday morning of the sixth full week of middle school, I found my way to Miss Mathews' homeroom and took my assigned seat opposite Sarah Kervick. I sit next to Sarah Kervick in five of my seven classes. My mother calls it fate. I call it administrative tampering at the highest level. You see, while Sarah has taken it upon herself to keep me safe from the criminal element at school, I am to make sure that her grade point average doesn't travel south of a 2.0 or C, which is the requirement for participation in the Greater Pelican View Amateur Figure Skating Association, otherwise known as the GPVAFSA.

Honestly, I don't know whose task is more difficult.

"Well, what did Gloria say?" she whispered as Miss Mathews carefully arranged herself in a seated position on the table near the whiteboard, her grade book at her side.

"She said you better get your costume or you won't have one in time for the exhibition," I whispered back. "Or the regionals!"

Sarah gripped the edge of her desk. "Not about that! About . . . you know . . . the other thing."

Was it a clear view of Miss Mathews' knees or Sarah mentioning "the other thing" that caused me to suddenly feel like my face had a tropical fever? Miss Mathews was a recent graduate of Michigan State University with a dual degree in English and science education. While I had no quarrel with her credentials, both her age and her style of dress made it difficult for me to think of her as a teacher.

In fact, it was Miss Mathews in a wrap skirt and sleeveless blouse that sent me to WebMD.com to find a remedy for the vessel-dilating response known as blushing. Blushing results from the severe dilation of the small blood vessels in the face. We blush when we're uncomfortable, or in response to undesired social attention. Blushing is most common during adolescence—yes, the middle-school years!—when social anxiety is at its peak. I'm sorry to report there is no cure for blushing, leading me to wonder how all this redirection of blood flow would affect my overall level of health.

I turned back to Sarah. "She said I should turn on the faucet, okay?"

"That's what I told you!" Sarah said, squeezing my arm like a python. She seemed to forget we were in the center of a crowded classroom with a teacher up front taking attendance.

"Samantha?" Miss Mathews cupped a hand behind her ear and leaned forward. "Do you have something to say to us?"

Sarah slumped down in her seat and glared at Miss Mathews.

"It's Sarah, not Samantha."

"Sarah?" Miss Mathews consulted her grade book. "I'm sorry, I was thinking of third period. Samantha Edwards sits in that seat third period."

"Whatever," Sarah responded.

Miss Mathews looked as if she'd hoped for more, so I added, "A completely natural mistake," and the roll taking continued.

"It's not like you can set the mood when football players are jostling through," I said to Sarah, keeping my voice low.

"We'll do it right after lunch, then. At that one by the gym. Nobody's over there after lunch." Sarah ran her hand through her long blond hair and sighed. "Just meet me there, okay?"

I had my doubts about the bathroom by the gym, but as FDR says, "It is common sense to take a method and try it. If it fails, admit it frankly and try another. But above all, try something."

For now, it was important to push aside thoughts of a restroom break and prepare for health class, which was taught by none other than our youthful homeroom teacher. Currently, we were finishing up our unit on environmental hazards, a subject in which I am quite interested. In fact, I would be a lively participant in health class if it weren't for Miss Mathews, who seemed to think that skirts above the knee, leotards, and low-rise khakis were appropriate teaching attire. It made me a bit wistful for Ms. Rita Linski, my fifth-grade teacher, whose polyester pantsuits just made me feel itchy.

I pulled my notebook with the color-coded vertical tabs that read TAINTED WATER, AIR POLLUTION, and PESTICIDES out of my backpack. At my dining-room table, I had assembled a similar notebook for Sarah Kervick while she amused herself trying to clamp a couple of chopsticks from Yen Ching, my mother's favorite takeout place, beneath her upper lip.

"Check it out," she'd said. "I'm a walrus."

"Where is your notebook?" I whispered to her now. "She's going to check it today!"

Sarah looked dreamily out the window, clearly in another world. Most likely it was a frosty one where figure skaters flew at dangerous speeds over the ice.

"What?"

"The notebook with all the handouts. It's worth fifteen percent of your grade!"

Sarah looked at me in confusion. Clearly, she hadn't read over the syllabus in preparation for class.

"Look in your backpack," I ordered her, yanking it out

from underneath her chair. Unfortunately, it was not zipped and the contents spilled into the aisle between us.

"Sarah? Franklin? The way you two go on, I'm beginning to think a presentation is called for. Our next unit will be: How to Tell If It's Really Love."

There was a burst of laughter and the sound of denim sliding over plastic as the entire class shifted in their seats to look at us. I lost all feeling in my fingers and my toes as the blood that belonged in other parts of my body rushed to my face. Ducking down, I yanked the notebook from the bottom of the pile and placed it on Sarah's desk.

All eyes, as they say, were upon us. Two of those eyes belonged to Glynnis Powell, a young woman of fine character whose attentions I hoped someday to enjoy. I imagined her pained confusion at that moment. Hadn't we exchanged tokens in the form of organic fruit rolls back in elementary school? What about those milk-money quarters I'd shined especially for her?

Sarah attempted to stuff the guts of her backpack under her seat before returning to her slouched position and shooting menacing glances at the kids who were still watching her. A Sarah Kervick stare is very effective at making students turn around.

"Thanks for nothin'," she hissed as Miss Mathews began her speech on the ninety-eight toxic chemicals in secondhand smoke.

# CHAPTER TWO

# The Remains of the Tray

Lunch at Pelican View Middle School was a very busy time for me. It may come as a surprise that this had nothing to do with eating. A great deal of my lunchroom time was devoted to what I call "blending." Caring about what others thought was a completely new sensation for me, but in middle school I quickly discovered that fitting in with my peers was as important to health promotion and risk avoidance as washing one's hands regularly and obeying the WALK indicators at busy intersections.

Why? Because sitting alone in the lunchroom marks you as easy prey. Tommy Williams, who was quickly developing a reputation as *the* practical joker of the sixth grade, routinely snatched the chairs out from underneath students who sat alone. A student on her own was also far more likely to have her lunch scavenged by a roving athlete.

Where were the caring adults who prevented these incidents? Except for Mr. Fiegel, our social studies teacher, they were closeted away in the teachers' lounge, enjoying adult conversation, filtered spring water from the office cooler, and the use of private bathroom facilities. That's where.

But Mr. Fiegel, it was rumored, had his eye on the assistant principal's job, so he volunteered to "maintain order" in the lunchroom. At the beginning of the lunch period, he pulled a stool up next to the condiment table. Tall and thin, with an Adam's apple that rivaled Ichabod Crane's, Mr. Fiegel perched on his stool and used a bullhorn to keep misbehaving students in line.

When a student broke a rule, Mr. Fiegel would flick on his bullhorn with a screech and bark into it: "Williams" or "Norton" or even "the gentleman in the soiled red T-shirt." If there was any doubt about the perpetrator of the crime, Mr. Fiegel would mark him with the ray of his infrared pointer pen, an instrument more commonly found in executive boardrooms during PowerPoint presentations. He would then refer to a cryptic list of lunchroom rules, such as: "only two cheeks to a seat," "no roving allowed," or "backpacks must be stowed securely."

I have repeatedly requested a written list of these lunchroom rules so that I might follow them. Every time I do this, I am told by Miss Rhonda, the school secretary, that they are in the process of being typed up. I am beginning to think Mr. Fiegel is flying by the seat of his pants, as my mother would say, with regard to these lunchroom rules. The clear lack of instructions, plus the fact that there was only one adult supervising almost two hundred sixth graders, added up to this: every boy for himself (or girl as the case may be).

So each time I entered the lunchroom, my primary goal was to band together with the only two students I knew who might be willing to shield me with a lunch tray during a food fight. The first was Bernie Lepner. Bernie was my next-door neighbor. Up until last year, Bernie was in the grade below me;

but due to a battery of intelligence tests he took in the spring, he had been encouraged to skip fifth grade entirely. My mother calls Bernie dreamy. Absentminded seems a more appropriate description. Bernie's mind is always on the characters he reads about in books or the epic medieval fantasy he is creating for future serialization. If you ask him about it, he will suddenly come alive and recall for you a recent battle or plot of murderous revenge, describing in detail the next chapter in his "quatrillionology."

Since we pack our lunches, Bernie and I usually meet at the entrance to the cafetorium, which is how everyone refers to our lunchroom since it also doubles as our auditorium. While Bernie is willing to take whatever seat is available, I prefer to look around a little first. In fact, I am often forced to reach out and grab Bernie's collar before he puts us in danger.

"Not there!"

"What? Why?"

"Bernie." I gestured in the direction he was heading. "Look at the aisles. Nothing but giant legs. This is where the football players sit."

"The football players? Where?"

Honestly, if Bernie were a rabbit, he'd cross open fields under a full moon. While it was true that they didn't have on the jerseys they wore on game days, it was hard to mistake a football player.

"Right over there. Next to the food-dispensing line, with its easy access to seconds. Oh, for heaven's sake, Bernie, look at them. They've been drinking hormone-laden milk since infancy. They could bench-press you."

"Okay, okay." Bernie turned in another direction and headed for a table in the corner.

I rushed to cut him off. "No, sorry. Not there, either."

Even he couldn't fail to see the reason this area was off-limits. The girls wore dark makeup under their eyes; the boys had chains dangling from their pockets, and hair that stood up in jagged rows. The entire table was wearing black.

Bernie sighed. "Why don't you pick, Franklin?"

"I'd be happy to." There was just one other location, aside from the football players and the future juvenile delinquents, that I wished to avoid. And that was the table that included boys who had not survived Coach Dilemming's summer basic-skills camp and, therefore, did not make it onto the football team. While I've no doubt they spent hours of their free time playing "first-person shooter" video games, these boys had no outlet for their anger during school hours.

Among them was Marvin Howerton, a student with whom I had a long history of entanglement, dating back to kinder-garten. There was something about sensitive, asymmetrical guys like me that incited Marvin Howerton to violence.

I located Marvin's table and then, using a quick geometric calculation, found a table in a low-traffic area that was farthest from the three points I most hoped to avoid. Keeping my elbows tucked close to my body, my lunch box in front of me, and a close eye on Bernie, I reached the table safely. Sliding into my seat, I stowed my backpack securely beneath it and breathed a sigh of relief.

"Hey, Bern. Hey, Franklin." Sarah Kervick slapped her tray down across from me.

Sarah was the second of my lunchroom partners. Despite the incident in homeroom earlier and her lack of etiquette in general; despite Bernie's lack of focus and his tendency to speak with his mouth full, Sarah and Bernie were my people. And I was grateful for them.

"Hello, everyone," I said cheerily, and lifted the lid on my insulated lunch box.

Without a word of explanation, I set a wrapped sandwich in the middle of the table before fanning the lid of my cooler back and forth to redirect the scent of Sarah Kervick—a mixture of stale secondhand cigarette smoke and tuna-noodle casserole. Bernie, too, set out a bag of chips, a deli pickle, and a corn dog between us. Our mothers had begun competing to make sure Sarah remained full until the end of the day. Most of these items would be scooped into her backpack for later consumption. Sarah had a fondness for school hot lunch that I could not fathom.

"Don't forget," I said to Sarah, "my mother wants you to remind your dad that she's taking you to get your skating costume this week."

Sarah flipped her hair back over her shoulders. She was wearing a white blouse, a V-neck sweater, and a pair of green corduroy pants, all purchased by my mother at the beginning of the school year. I could just see her trying to formulate an excuse.

"My mother said to tell you, and I quote: 'We're really pushing it. We have to go this week unless Sarah wants to make her first public skating appearance in the nude.'"

Even though it was a direct quote, the word *nude* still made the blood vessels in my cheeks dilate.

"I could perform in my warm-up suit," Sarah offered, as if we hadn't been over this a thousand times.

"And the judges would think you didn't care and give you low marks."

"What about . . ."

"You have to wear a skirt or a dress. All the girls do."

"Your mom doesn't."

"That's how much you know. She's going out to buy a dress tonight."

"Is not."

"Tree nymphs are always nude," Bernie said, biting down on his own deli pickle and releasing vinegar fumes into the air. "At least in my story."

Sarah hunched over her casserole and stabbed it with a fork. "Where were we, Bern?" she said, as if our conversation was already over.

I knew she'd heard me.

"In the Malogon Forest," Bernie replied, mouth full of pickle. "At the edge of the Jun Dun Plain. The Sandroheens, a small band of Dorgon Trolls, are making their way through the forest, hacking at the undergrowth with their double-broad tonken blades—"

"They were looking for the queen," Sarah broke in. "They knew she was captured somewhere nearby."

"Right." Bernie rewarded Sarah with a big grin. "Dorgon Trolls have a very keen sense of smell. They were tracking her."

While the two of them crashed through the underbrush of the Malogon Forest, I stayed behind in the lunchroom, continuing with a quest of my own. I found the third long lunch table and traveled along it with my eyes—noting infractions along the way that included a blob of mustard launched from a plastic spoon and condiment packages stuffed into backpacks. It seemed that Mr. Fiegel was falling down on the job today.

I kept this up until my eyes alighted on their prize. Glynnis Powell. A creature of habit, Glynnis always sat at the near end of table number three.

She was surrounded by girls I did not know, since they'd come from other elementary schools. It was a mystery to me why Glynnis sat with these girls, who seemed more like a flighty bunch of sparrows than serious students the way they always laughed at the same time and covered their mouths in shock, whispering furiously. I could tell in an instant that she was not comfortable there. Her excellent posture was a little stiff, her smile a bit forced. Only a boy who had chosen her as the object of his affections would notice these things, I told myself. Only I, Franklin Delano Donuthead, understood her distress.

I watched her politely touch the corners of her mouth with her napkin and imagined that I was a Dorgon Troll, distinguishing her clean, Ivory-soap smell from Bernie's deli pickles, from the odor of Mr. Kervick's smoke that clung to Sarah's hair, from the combined stench of a dozen mayonnaise-slathered sandwiches that had been sitting unrefrigerated in poorly ventilated lockers for at least four hours, and I sighed happily.

As if to make my bliss complete, Glynnis' eyes met mine, and she smiled before looking down at her lap. Did this mean that the events of this morning had been understood in their proper context and I was forgiven?

Suddenly a hand was thrust in my face.

"C'mon, we gotta get to the john," Sarah said, snapping her fingers.

# Positive Rewards, Positive Results

We chose the bathroom by the gym because it was on the opposite side of the school from the lunchroom and less likely to be populated during those hours. As we reached the entrance, she pushed open the swinging door and glanced inside.

"Uhhh . . . anybody here?" she asked. When no one answered, she dropped her backpack on the floor and tilted her head to indicate that the coast was clear. Knowing there was no safer place to stow my backpack, I was forced to hand it over to Sarah for safekeeping.

This I did with my head down. After all, I'd just had a mature moment with Glynnis Powell. What would Glynnis think if she knew I required Sarah Kervick as a "lookout" and the senseless waste of tap water to make it possible for me to pee?

I had to put this behind me.

Pelican View Middle is the oldest building in the school district. Rather than urinals with dividers between them—as some more modern facilities use to give the appearance of privacy—the creators of this building had constructed what could almost be called a fountain in the middle of the room. The wall opposite the door was flanked by sinks with metal mirrors above them. Two stalls had been constructed in the far corner, clearly meant to handle bathroom needs no sane middle-school boy would even attempt. There were also a few urinals along the wall to our left. But it was clearly this huge porcelain bowl with twelve trickles of water running into each of its twelve drains that was meant to handle most of the bathroom traffic.

Normally, I just used the stall. But today, for some reason, I felt a surge of confidence. Today, I would add my stream to The Bowl.

I approached it in a relaxed manner and unzipped my pants. Closing my eyes, I focused on the faint sound of trickling water. Everything was fine. Things were going, on the whole, quite well. I even allowed myself to visualize the moment just after I'd successfully concluded my business at The Bowl and was washing my hands thoroughly under a gushing faucet.

"How long is this gonna take?" Sarah Kervick had pushed the door halfway open, and I caught a glimpse of her head in the mirror. I bent double to cover myself.

"It's not like I can see anything, Franklin," she said. "Plus, I'm not interested." Her gaze fell on the sinks.

"What did I say about the water? Will you listen for once? I gotta get to my locker!"

"Your tone of voice is not helping," I replied, zipping up again.

She banged through the door into the room. "Just get in the stall, okay?"

I walked with dignity through the open stall door and slid the latch into place.

Sarah Kervick proceeded to turn on every faucet in the room, simulating a trip on the cruise boat *Maid of the Mist* as it went directly under Niagara Falls. Not that I have ever been. I did stand a safe distance away from the falls on a concrete embankment in the care of a nice Royal Canadian Mounted Police officer once while my mother and her best friend, Penny, took the trip.

Even at the time, I wanted to wet my pants as Mother and Penny disappeared into the clouds of churning foam. I was picturing life in some Canadian orphanage, competing for sunlight through barred windows with homeless urchins and street toughs.

Thus, Gloria's advice worked like a charm. I was just zipping up for the second time when I heard Sarah's voice again.

"What are you lookin' at? Never seen a girl before?"

"Uh . . . not in the boys' bathroom."

"You got a problem with that?"

"Uh . . . no."

"I could maybe nail your eyelids to your cheekbones and give you a problem."

"That's okay. . . ."

I heard the sound of feet beating it, and I peeked out the stall door.

"You better hurry up, Franklin. I'm warning you, just one verse or I'm dragging you out of here."

I soaped up and began humming the "Happy Birthday" song to myself. I used to go through it three times—two if I added the "how old are you" verse—to completely clean *and* disinfect, but Sarah Kervick, middle-school bell times, and the desire to catch a glimpse of Glynnis Powell in the hallway had me soap-lather-and-rinsing in record time these days.

As Sarah pulled me out into the hall, we practically tripped over the giant feet of Marvin Howerton and Bryce Jordan, who stood over us, examining our backpacks, which—to my disgust—Sarah had tossed *on the floor.*

Sarah tried to ignore them, hunching her shoulders and bending at the knees to pick up our packs. Despite her tough-talking ways, Sarah Kervick does not like to fight.

But Marvin put his foot on her hand.

"Me and Bryce got a bet on what you were doing in there," Marvin said. "Spill it, so he can pay up."

Sarah Kervick weighed, maybe, one-half a Marvin Howerton. She yanked her hand out from under his shoe and straightened up.

"You wanna square off, that's fine," she said, squinting up at him. "But I'm keepin' my nose clean at school."

She tried to sidestep him but he boxed her in, pushing her back into a row of metal lockers.

When will Marvin Howerton learn? If you value your life, you should never push Sarah Kervick and remain in striking range. Her countermove was quicker than the eye could register. Before Bryce and I could react, Marvin was bent double. Within seconds, she had ahold of our backpacks and was yanking on my long arm.

Over her shoulder, she said, "So make an appointment."

In our haste to get away, we almost bumped into Mr.

Herman, the school custodian, who rounded the corner with a cavernous waste can on cast-iron wheels. He was, no doubt, heading for the Dumpster just outside the utility entrance. My fear of Marvin Howerton was replaced by my fear of lunchroom remains, and I instinctively set a new course as far away from Mr. Herman as I could.

But when he saw Sarah, he stopped. Reaching out his hand, he placed it on her shoulder. They looked at each other for a long while.

"Okay?" was all he said.

*Not okay*, I thought. Nobody touches Sarah Kervick without her permission. I cringed and arranged my arms so that they could protect my body from flying garbage.

But nothing happened. Sarah used her chin to indicate Bryce and Marvin behind us. Mr. Herman nodded in a way that suggested Marvin's condition was regrettable, but he understood it had been necessary. The hall began to fill with students.

"What was that about?" I asked as we were sucked into the stream, girls darting back and forth like dragonflies in their attempt to communicate as much as possible in the four-minute time frame.

Sarah shrugged. "I know him, that's all. He and my dad worked for the same roofing guy last summer. He lives near us."

"Well," I replied. I had no idea what else to say. You would think it worth mentioning that Sarah was on a shoulder-squeezing level with our school's custodian. "Don't forget about Thursday after school," I called out as she headed off to her locker. "My mother is leaving a note for your dad about it today."

Normally, when the parents of middle-school students arrange an outing for their children, they communicate with one another via the device known as a telephone, invented in 1897. Ninety-eight percent of American homes have at least one phone. Over 70 percent have computers. The Kervicks had neither. To make arrangements with Sarah Kervick, we had to actually *go* to her home. You might think her father would welcome us warmly, given the time, attention, and money my mother has lavished on his daughter. But this was not the case. He often pretended not to be home, even when it was obvious by the blaring television that he was.

After school, Bernie and I stood on the sidewalk, waiting for the nice lady in the neon pinafore to signal that it was safe to cross. Just before I stepped off the curb, however, my mother's van pulled up alongside us.

"Did Sarah get on the bus already?" she asked by way of greeting.

As if in answer to her question, several buses rattled by, spewing exhaust.

"Oh hi, Julia." At the sight of my mother, Bernie tried to return to reality. He once described for me in detail the Sandroheen queen. It came as no surprise that she was the spitting image of my mother. How did she earn such loyalty? From the time he was four, my mother gave Bernie free reign under our front porch. Rebeltown, as he called it, was Bernie's favorite place to hang out. And his favorite visitor was Julia Donuthead. All the cowboys shot their guns in the air when she came around.

"I'll give you guys a ride home," she said, patting the front passenger seat. "Guests up front. Hop in, Bern."

As soon as we were captive and fastened into our seats, she added: "But I still have to tell Sarah's dad about tomorrow."

Off we sped toward Sarah Kervick's trailer, which was in just the opposite direction of our own tidy, safe, bungalow-style ranch. For Bernie, this was a delightful turn of events. He now had the promise of a long ride that would result in his arriving at home without the bother of obeying traffic signals or tripping over broken pavement.

I was less thrilled by the prospect of a visit to Sarah Kervick's home. Everything about her home environment—from the trailer that sat crookedly on cinder blocks, to the assorted rusting auto parts that surrounded the cars Mr. Kervick was fixing up, to his attempts to get my mother to hook up the adults-only cable package "on the low," to his *unchained* dogs—had a very bad effect on my blood pressure. Sarah always provided a measure of protection against these dangers, but she had taken the bus, so we were sure to arrive before her.

What to do? My mother and Bernie were already involved in a discussion of Jun Dun geography, so I figured I might as well sink into a pleasant contemplation of my own: how to calmly invite Glynnis Powell to sit with us at lunch without the noticeable redirection of blood flow to my craniofacial muscles. Surely our conversation topics, which ranged from medieval fantasy, to the physics of a rear-entry single-lutz skate jump, to the nutritional merits of eating fruit with or without the skin, would be more interesting to her than whatever piece of gossip the girls were gnawing on at her lunch table.

Under my breath, I tried out a few oh-so-casual openers that might lead elegantly to an invitation.

"Oh hello, Glynnis," I might say as we filed out of health class together. "Wasn't that a fascinating session on the toxicity of cigarettes?"

*No. Bad form to bring up toxicity and then lunch. Begin again.*

Manage to get to door frame at same time and say with surprise: "Glynnis. Hello! Where are you off to?" And, having memorized her schedule and *knowing* she will say "Spanish," reply with a chipper, "Oh. *Sí. Hasta la vista. En la cafetería?*"

What if I raised my eyebrows slightly? Maybe a slight incline of the head? Was there a Spanish word for *cafetorium*?

I decided this was an excellent way to proceed because Glynnis could translate my line in her next class, saving us both the embarrassment of a simultaneous blush.

But my planning session was interrupted by the van's bone-jarring arrival on what can only politely be called Sarah Kervick's street (though the word *street* brings to mind pavement, curbs, and dividing lines, and this narrow dirt lane with potholes the size of bowling balls did not do that).

Bernie didn't come back to earth until the car was parked and one of Sarah's hounds had leapt up to press his face against the window, making a most unpleasant noise with his toenails on the passenger-side door. Pressing the latch on the glove compartment, Bernie pulled out a box of Thompson Treats: Specially Formulated Reward Behavior Dog Biscuits.

"He knows you're here, Julia," he said calmly, smiling up at her from underneath his bangs and handing over the box.

Thompson Treats had been developed by Pelican View's own Trevor Thompson. My mother had heard him speak from the air-conditioning duct at the forty-second Chow Hound franchise, where she was at work installing cable lines so employees could watch Animal Planet in the break room. His talk was entitled "Positive Rewards, Positive Results."

She leapt out of the car, box in hand, and out came the second, more timid, of Sarah's dogs to sit and beg at the coveted spot by my mother's right hand. One was named Pretzel and one Zero, though I could never remember which was which. Together, they stirred up a cloud of dust with their rears and tails as they sat, impatiently, eyes on my mother's right hand, waiting for a Thompson Treat and a pat on the head.

Bernie jumped out of the van and joined the fracas. I preferred to remain in my place, though when Mr. Kervick appeared, wiping his oil-blackened hands on a grimy rag, I did crack my window.

Sometimes I try to imagine what my own father looks like. We have never met him. He just . . . well . . . provided the ingredients. I don't know how to talk about this to people who don't already know. Some people think a child who is the product of a mom and a sperm donor is just plain weird. If only they knew—there are millions of us in schools across America!

It's like my mother wanted to make a cake and she went to

the store to get some flour. While I might have chosen stone-ground, organic, whole-wheat pastry flour from a family-run cooperative in Wisconsin, she probably took whatever was closest to hand, even if it meant the on-sale store brand dangerously near its sell-by date.

"I wanted a healthy guy" is all she'll tell me.

But my mother wanted a baby, not a cake. This required sperm, not flour. And since I bear very little resemblance to my mother in either looks or personality, she may have grabbed the container that advertised: "sensitive-intelligent-asymmetrical-immaculate male" in her rush to get the whole business over with. As she is repeatedly reminding me, what she wanted was: "normal-dog-loving-athletic sports fan." But I can hardly be held responsible for my own genes, now can I?

Whatever I had in mind for my father had nothing in common with the man who was at this very moment standing across from my mother. He wore a denim work jacket over a stained muscle shirt. His lips seemed permanently clenched around an unfiltered cigarette; his balding head had been overexposed to the sun for many a year. In short, the man was a walking bundle of risk factors for a variety of cancers, including skin, throat, lung, and stomach lining.

"Whatcha got today?" he asked, expertly keeping the cigarette in place while he talked. My mother was still kneeling, rewarding the dogs with her presence and scratching them behind the ears. She looked up at him.

"Just wanted to let you know, Sarah's first competition is in three weeks."

"That so?"

"There will be an exhibition the week before, sort of like a dress rehearsal. I know how much she wants you to come."

"Might have to work," he said, concentrating now on the oil between his fingers and digging in with the rag. In addition to fixing up cars and roofing during the summer, Sarah's father did temp work at the door-panel factory over in Marshfield.

My mother set her box of Thompson Treats on the hood of the van and waited. She wanted an answer. She wasn't going to let Mr. Kervick off the hook. Without treats in the immediate vicinity of their noses, the dogs whined and started jumping up on my mother. Bernie tried to distract them with an empty fist held just above their heads, but that made them jump higher and paw the air.

"Get on!" Mr. Kervick growled, swiping at them with his rag.

Was it the tone of his voice or the threat of a swat that drove them to run, ears back, tails tucked between their legs, into the shed where Mr. Kervick kept his tools?

My mother folded her arms. So much for positive rewards.

"Back in the car, Bern." After Bernie had slammed the door, she continued: "Well, I'll have her Thursday after school, getting fitted for her skating costume . . . and a sandwich after, if it's all right by you."

Mr. Kervick had a hard time setting his eyes anywhere, and—I'd observed—he had a particularly hard time looking my mother in the eye.

But now he dropped his cigarette in the dirt and stepped in closer, lowering his voice. I couldn't make out all he said, only the snatches: "You done a lot for Sarah, her not having a ma and all . . ." and ". . . take up work with my brother over in Muskegon . . ."

When he finished, he seemed to be waiting for her to say something. It was as if he'd doled out so many more words than usual, my mother owed him a few back. But she didn't answer. She just shrugged her shoulders and got back in the van, closing the door, turning the key in the ignition, and placing her hands on the steering wheel, all with the slow, controlled movements that told me my mother was trying her best not to fly off the handle.

We passed Sarah's bus in a cloud of dust on the way to the main road.

Finally, when we were back on pavement, my mother turned to Bernie: " 'We never stay in one place long.' That's what he said." She continued, imitating Mr. Kervick's raspy voice. " 'It might do ya to remember that.' "

"I'm sorry, Julia . . ." Bernie had been out of conversation range, lost among the tall grass of the Jun Dun Plain. "What were you saying?"

"Was that supposed to be a threat?" she asked him.

Before I could contribute a resounding "Yes!" from the backseat, my mother twisted the volume on the radio, and we were awash in the unsafe decibel levels of her favorite classic-rock station.

# CHAPTER FOUR

# Marked as an Unfortunate

As if this wasn't enough extracurricular activity for one day, my mother and I set out after dinner to run a few errands. This included picking up her work boots from the repair shop and purchasing a dress.

Paul had invited my mother to the fish fry at the Lions Club on Friday night. He wanted her to wear a dress. This doesn't seem odd unless you know my mother. As soon as she started paying her own way, Julia Donuthead stopped wearing dresses.

"I just don't prefer them," she'd respond when challenged. Her willingness to buy one now told me that things with Paul were taking a very serious turn.

As soon as I got in the van, I noticed something odd suctioned to the dashboard. It looked like a test tube.

"What is this?" I asked, pointing to it.

"What is what?" My mother pulled out into traffic.

"This." I reached over and put her hand on it.

"Oh . . . um, nothing." She pulled it off the dash with a *thwock* and stuffed it in her glove compartment. *All while accelerating to forty-five miles per hour.*

"I still saw it," I said, waiting for the explanation.

"It's a vase, all right, Detective Donuthead?"

"If it's a vase, why doesn't it have flowers in it?"

"I found you a community-service activity," she announced as we turned into the parking lot of Alpine Shoe Repair.

I sighed. "Fine." As with a number of things going on lately, no further explanation would be provided. "I thought *I* was supposed to find me a community-service job."

After carefully considering my choices, I had decided that Sarah and I could stuff envelopes for the Land Conservancy. They had a nice renovated office on Main Street. The worst outcome I could think of was a paper cut, *and* it wouldn't require much of Sarah's concentration.

"I met up with Mack Putnam down at Perkins' Drug Store, and he said Grace in the library could use some help reshelving the books. Her knees aren't what they used to be, and the picture books are all down by the floor."

"Are we speaking of Mrs. Boardman in the Pelican View Elementary library?"

"Right. Sorry. Mr. Putnam, your old principal, wants you to help Mrs. Boardman, your old librarian."

"Library aide," I corrected her. "But I can't go back to Pelican View Elementary. I'm a sixth grader."

We'd pulled into the department-store parking lot, and my mother unlocked the doors.

"Oh, Franklin, it's not a hard job. It's better than touching germy kids. There's almost no possibility of being struck by lightning or held hostage at gunpoint. Just make my life easy for once and do it without the endless commentary, okay?"

"Well, I . . ." I could see she was dead serious. My mother gets very stressed out when she goes shopping. "Okay."

"Now grit your teeth and help me find a dress."

"Okay," I said quietly, and I offered no commentary about the fact that while there is nothing statistically dangerous about the ladies' section of a department store, I, too, feel uneasy when I'm in one. This may be due to bad memories of trying to keep track of my mother as she power walked through the store. Now that I could see above the racks, however, this was less of an issue.

As we headed to Misses' Dresses, I realized the problem. Everywhere you looked, you were reminded of . . . well, women. Ladies' pajamas, ladies' workout wear, ladies' *lingerie*.

I saw a man about my mother's age looking similarly uncomfortable, pressed into one of those little chairs outside the dressing room. A woman came out in a pair of dress pants, lifted up the tails of her blouse and turned in a circle.

"How does this look from the back?" she said. "I'm going for professional. It's an interview."

I froze in place. Was she talking to me? This would be a difficult question to answer tactfully.

He mumbled something and I hurried along.

My mother was attacking the sale rack, pulling out one dress after the other and frowning. I began to search the next size up and pulled out a perfectly nice shirtdress in neutral brown.

"What about this?"

"Oh, please, Franklin. I don't want to look like the lady at the license bureau. It's a dance."

"I thought it was a fish fry!"

"It's a fish fry *and* a dance."

"Is it . . . formal?" I asked, hoping not. If Paul had invited my mother to the prom for forty-somethings, things were even worse than they seemed.

"No."

"Aren't these the summer dresses?" I asked, fingering the material. "You'll get goose bumps if you wear these in October, Mother. Goose bumps are not attractive on a woman your age. Maybe something wool . . ."

My mother had pulled out a black dress covered with sprays of pollen-producing wildflowers.

"You can't wear that. It doesn't have any sleeves."

"Yes it does. They're called cap sleeves."

I eyed her suspiciously.

"Don't look like that. We have *InStyle* in the break room at work."

"Well . . . try it on then," I urged her, against my better judgment. There was something to be said for just getting it over with.

I took my seat opposite the gentleman assigned to comment on how his wife fit into business attire.

He looked over at me and shrugged. "Tough duty, eh?"

I nodded. It was indeed.

"Tell you what, you take my wife and I'll take your mom. That way things'll go easier for us at home."

At that very moment, his wife peeked out of the dressing room and proceeded to model another outfit.

"What in the Sam Hill . . . ?"

"It's called a 'skort.' It's a cross between a skirt and shorts." She walked farther away so that we could get a better look.

"Give me the damage," she said, turning around.

The man across the aisle raised his eyebrows as if asking me to live up to my end of the bargain. I tried to formulate something positive, but the only phrase that came to mind was "elastic limit." I was saved from further embarrassment by my mother's appearance in the doorway. She walked past us *barefoot* and turned around.

The man in the opposite chair whistled softly and said to his wife, "Do they have one of those in your size?"

The woman eyed my mother critically. She tugged on the dress, went around back, and finished zipping the zipper.

"Stand up straight and own it, honey," the woman said. "This dress fits you like a glove."

My mother laughed and put her hands to her face, embarrassed. She had taken her hair out of its ponytail, and it fell down around her shoulders. Her long, muscled arms were still tan. The dress, tight along her rib cage, flared out and fell in soft folds just above her ankles.

There was something about the way she laughed, like a middle-school girl, and how she kept rising up on the balls of her feet that made me realize my mother was once young herself.

"Well, Franklin?" she asked.

I said the only thing that came to mind: "You look pretty."

• • •

Paul's pickup was parked smack in the middle of the driveway when we got home.

"Will this day never end?" I mumbled into the door as I stepped out of the van and braced myself for a clap on the shoulder.

"Hey, babe." Paul, who'd been sitting on the doorstep, jumped up to greet us.

"Hey. I thought you were working tonight."

"Got off a little early."

I studied the tips of my shoes while they kissed.

"So?" My mother unlocked the front door and held it open for us. I hurried through. In his excitement to see my mother, Paul had forgotten his usual greeting to me.

"Well, I stopped by Bert's Surplus to get some of that baling twine for all those pallets we got out back behind the ice rink, and I picked up an item for Franklin here."

Since he was behind me, Paul's hand clap caught me completely by surprise. I staggered into the hallway, trying to stay upright.

"Well, isn't that funny? Because we were out getting something for you, too."

"At LaVeen's?" Taking my mother's shopping bag, Paul pressed it all over with his fingers. "No way, Franklin!"

He lifted his hand in a high-five gesture. I was discovering that this was how my mother's boyfriend bonded with people. I braced my feet and raised my hand up and away from my body.

"You got your mother to buy a dress for the dance? Way to go!"

*Slap!*

"Well," he said. "Are you going to try it on for me?"

"Not on your life, mister. You can wait."

I bent down to remove my shoes, hoping Paul would follow my example.

"I figured." As he pulled my mother close, I was forced to make another thorough study of my footwear.

"So what did you get Franklin?"

"Oh." Paul pulled a handful of wool out of his jacket pocket and lobbed it at me. "Your mom told me you got the dreaded desk in Spansky's class."

I caught the material and stretched it out.

"Go on. Try it on."

"What exactly is it?" I asked him.

"It's a ski mask."

My mother started laughing. "Oh, Paul."

"I'm serious. It's gonna give you maximum protection. It was Hank Niemeyer who got that desk when I was at Pelican View Middle. Him and another kid. I don't know what happened to the other guy, but I see Hank every once in a while at the harness races and he still has a twitch.

"Try it on, Franklin," my mother said, chewing her lip to keep from laughing.

"I prefer to wash it first," I said, trying to imagine myself in sixth-grade science in the headgear most popular among bank robbers and terrorists.

"Yeah, that's okay. It's pretty much one-size-fits-all. But don't put it in the dryer. That's one hundred percent wool."

Maybe I'd better explain. It has always been my habit to sit at the front of the classroom. Studies have shown that scholastic achievement is directly linked to how close you sit to the teacher. Criminal activity is far less likely to occur in the front of the classroom than at the back. So, while Sarah Kervick found a seat that was wedged between an actual skeleton and a glass case containing jars of human organs(!) in formaldehyde solution on the first day of science class, I sat at one of the gleaming black lab tables just opposite Mr. Spansky's desk. While this proved to be the best seat possible for achieving mental improvement and risk avoidance, it was *not* the right location for health promotion.

On the first day of class, Mr. Spansky pinched the ends of his bow tie so that they stood out from his lab coat in perfect symmetry. He walked around his desk and leaned against it. He was a mere three feet away. Leaning back, he removed two pairs of safety glasses from the drawer in his desk and handed them across the lab table to me and to Bernie, who'd arrived late and taken the only seat left, which just so happened to be at my table.

At first, I was pleased, thinking that my reputation had preceded me and Mr. Spansky was trying to respect my wishes regarding risk avoidance. Bernie held up the safety glasses as if to ask, *Has this already been covered?* Since class was about to begin, I could only answer with a shrug.

We put on our safety glasses. As it turned out, just in time.

"Good morning, and welcome to my—Mr. Spansky's— sixth-grade science class."

Note, if you will, how many words in that sentence contain the letter *s*. As soon as his brief declaration was complete, the lab table in front of us was covered in shining bubbles of Mr. Spansky's spit, horrifically highlighted by the table's dark color. Extracting a spray bottle from his front pocket, Mr. Spansky quickly dispatched the mess with a spritz and a paper-towel wipe down.

Bernie and I exchanged quick glances through our violated glasses as the classroom around us broke up laughing.

"Due to a deficiency in my palate, I am unable to contain all of my saliva in my mouth when I speak. This necessitates—*squirt, squirt, rub, rub*—the use of certain antiseptic measures. I beg your understanding."

By the time his little speech was completed, I was crouching beneath the table. Hadn't the man lived with his disability long enough to know that words like *necessitates* should be permanently removed from his vocabulary?

Needless to say, Bernie and I had snagged the seats for the entire semester. Though Paul's heart may have been in the right place—I'm still not entirely sure he wasn't making fun of me—even I could see that wearing a ski mask in Mr. Spansky's class would amount to social suicide.

So I learned to develop my own precautions. At the end of each class period, as I bent over to return my materials to my backpack, I quickly wiped my face with antibacterial wet wipes, the sort that mothers stow in their baby's diaper bag. I also had a small Mercurochrome stick for direct hits. While using "the stick" left an orange mark, I relied on the general chaos between classes to let disinfecting occur, and then wiped it off at my locker just before lunch.

I developed my emergency hygiene plan just in time. Not

long after the year began, we launched into a unit on single-celled organisms. I should note that science teachers seldom refer to the building blocks of the universe in the singular: not atom, but atoms; not electron, but electrons . . . protons, neutrons, strands of DNA. But even a long speech on single-celled organisms could not compare to the shock I received in the cafetorium that Wednesday.

Our small band had assembled and lunch was proceeding as usual, with Bernie relating another installment, this time about the Dorgon Trolls' sworn enemies—the dreaded dragons of Lairding—while Sarah Kervick chewed on rubbery chicken fingers and asked for clarifications in the action before swallowing. She had just opened her mouth again to speak when I, Franklin Delano Donuthead, did something I try very hard not to do. And that is: act on impulse.

I had decided the evening before that speaking to Glynnis Powell might be easier if I first practiced being *within* speaking distance. After that, a casual "hi" in passing would be the next logical step. My plan had been to spend the next few weeks carefully determining the locations we would most likely "bump into" each other.

But as I sat there with my organic yogurt untouched in front of me, I started hearing voices inside my head.

Voice of FDR: *Men are not prisoners of fate, Franklin, but only prisoners of their own minds.*

Voice of Franklin: *Stay where you are and eat your yogurt. You haven't achieved the USDA-recommended amount of calcium yet today.*

Voice of FDR: *It isn't sufficient just to want—you've got to ask yourself what you are going to do to get the things you want.*

I was so caught up in the conversation going on in my head that I said out loud, "But it's game day. I already have a plan!"

Sarah and Bernie looked over at me with surprise.

On game days, Pelican View football players wore their jerseys. Today was our first home game. My fear was that seeing the players in their red-and-white jerseys might have the same effect on Marvin Howerton that a piece of red silk has on a bull. He *might* look for ways to channel his aggression off the field, especially after the run-in we'd had the day before. My game-day plan was to wear dark colors and keep a low profile, so today was *not* the best day to be roaming the lunch area.

"Quick, where is Marvin?" I asked Bernie and Sarah.

They just kept staring, as if I'd said, *Where is the Martian?*

"How'm I supposed to know that?" Sarah Kervick answered, finally.

"I just thought . . . maybe . . ."

"I should put *him* in my book," Bernie said. "He could be one of the bog monsters."

"Good idea. Then we can kill him off."

As they put their heads together and plotted Marvin's demise in the swamps of the Malogon Forest, I continued to scan the lunchroom until I located the here-and-now Marvin Howerton, sitting with his back to us, his feet up on the table.

So it seemed safe to set out in the opposite direction on my quest for a crisp white blouse; a modest, knee-length checked skirt, or even a stone-washed denim kerchief.

As I walked, I scanned the lunchroom masses without success.

*Could she be ill?* I wondered. *Absent for a dental appointment?*

It was then I received the shock of my life; for there in front of me, in the place Glynnis normally occupied, sat a girl in a cheerleading uniform. As I stared at her back, covered in Pelican View Panther, reality began to sink in.

The intensity of my gaze caused Glynnis to shift in her seat. "Oh, Franklin," she said, covering her mouth with a napkin, as it still contained remnants of her whole-wheat organic pretzel twists.

"Glynnis," I said, too shocked even to dilate. "You're a cheerleader."

Glynnis glanced quickly at her seatmates, all festooned in red and white, with shockingly short, thigh-baring skirts.

"Hey, I've seen you somewhere before. What's your name?" one of the girls asked.

I almost reminded Rebecca Foster—for that was the name embroidered on her uniform—that the recommended way to introduce yourself, according to etiquette expert Miss Emily Post, is to state your name along with "It's nice to meet you." And not to blurt out rudely: "What's your name?"

However, I did not want to escalate the level of tension that already existed, so I simply answered her question: "Franklin Donuthead."

"Wait a minute. You're not a skater."

"No."

"Then why are you coming to my house tomorrow? *Donuthead* is on our calendar."

I had no idea what Rebecca was talking about. I looked helplessly at Glynnis. Were these really the sort of girls she chose to be friends with?

"No wait," said another cheerleader—Vivvy Heinz—whose mother allowed her to wear blue eye shadow and pink lip gloss to school. "You're the one who ducks under the table in science class."

Simultaneously, four cheerleaders covered their mouths and giggled.

Not Rebecca Foster. She continued to stare at me. "So what's that orange thing on your forehead?"

I touched my forehead lightly, realizing at once that I had forgotten to remove the Mercurochrome at my locker. Why had Bernie and Sarah failed to point this out to me? Was making Marvin Howerton an entrée for the dragons of Lairding more important than my reputation?

I stared back at the cheerleaders. There seemed to be nothing to do but confess.

"That would be Mercurochrome. I've gotten pretty good at dodging him, but Mr. Spansky does score a direct hit on occasion."

Six more hands flew to their mouths. I had the attention of the whole table now. I failed to see why my troubles with Mr. Spansky were so funny. I *did not* fail to see the look of distress on Glynnis' face.

Once again, reality hit me full force. She was ashamed of me—the poor unfortunate who'd been spit on by our science teacher and so become the laughingstock of her new friends. How I managed to stumble back to my own table I do not know. Even Bernie, who normally failed to read the subtle nonverbal cues of others, was shocked into silence by my pale expression.

"Franklin," he said, finally. "Are you okay?"

"All my hopes are dashed," I replied, sinking into my chair. "Why? *Why* didn't you tell me that I still had Mercurochrome on my forehead?"

Sarah Kervick swallowed the last of her chocolate milk and wiped her mouth on her sleeve. "That orange stuff?" She looked over at Bernie.

"It's been there before, Franklin," Bernie said matter-of-factly. "We thought you knew."

# Helping Out Hope

Every object has a center of gravity through which the laws of the earth and its magnetic forces act. I think it is safe to say that, most of the time, Sarah Kervick defies gravity.

For example, an object will remain stable as long as its center of gravity is directly over its base. For a skater, that means directly over the weight-bearing foot. Watching the other girls, it was easy to tell when their center of gravity shifted. Some were able to resist the pull of gravity by leaning in the other direction. Others fell. Repeatedly.

But Sarah Kervick's body seemed as finely calibrated as the ancient Egyptian scales of justice. At first, when she turned her skates out and leaned back into a spread eagle, I cringed with the knowledge of what happens to an unstable object. But when I opened my eyes, I found her gliding over the ice, a beatific look on her face, as if the invisible hand of Isaac Newton were pushing on the small of her back.

Normally, I was not recruited to observe the highly dangerous activity known as contract ice, where up to twenty-five skaters, most of them girls between the ages of ten and eighteen, pay for the chance to practice their routines. Twenty-five girls skating in twenty-five different directions is enough to bring about heart palpitations in the most seasoned air-traffic controller. But my mother's schedule on certain days made my attendance necessary, and I was told to do my homework in the "snack area" and *not* request that the table be sanitized more than one time. With Sarah just weeks away from her first exhibition, it seemed like the ice arena was becoming my second home.

My mother was rarely around during these sessions. As soon as we arrived at the rink, she would disappear into the girls' locker room, emerging near the end of Sarah's practice flushed and, obviously, worn out from the exertion. She told me there was a ballet barre and some weights in there that the girls used for warming up. Why not take advantage of the facilities?

"A strong core prevents injuries," she explained, imitating coach Debbi's heavy Swedish accent. It sounded suspiciously to me like she was trying to improve her statistics for Paul.

There were times when my mother felt bad about her neglectful behavior toward her only child and compensated by picking up little gifts for me during her workday. Most recently, I'd scored the updated edition of *Live Safely in a Dangerous World.* So I didn't dare tell her that I actually enjoyed the time I watched Sarah.

It all began a few months ago when Sarah took a bad spill while practicing a Salchow. She pulled herself up, skated over to the edge of the rink, and waved me closer.

"Franklin, did you know that was going to happen?" she shouted over the plastic barrier.

I nodded yes. Of course I did. Sarah had pressed down too hard on her toe pick, and that slowed her down. She tried to make up for it by cranking around the jump, but that just threw her off balance.

"You think you can still do that thing we did in baseball?"

"I'm afraid you need to be a bit more specific than 'that thing' . . . ?" I shouted back, getting a couple of slanty-sideways glances from hovering mothers. Distracting the skaters was frowned upon. I started down the bleacher steps.

"Where you know what's going to happen . . . remember?" Sarah said as we met at the opening of the rink.

When Sarah Kervick played outfield for Pelican View Elementary's Modern Hardware Team, I enjoyed predicting—and then conveying to her via agreed-upon hand signals—in what direction and how far the ball would travel, so that she could be waiting to meet it when it fell to the ground.

Still, I didn't see how knowing she would fall helped her. "It happens in an instant. There's no time to warn you."

Sarah tugged at the sleeves of her warm-up jacket. "Right. But I'll get smarter, see? If you teach me?"

I nodded. I did.

She tossed me the jacket and held out her hand. "Partners. Okay?"

We shook on it and I returned to my seat in the bleachers.

So, while my mother sweated it out in the locker room, I got my own share of cardiovascular exercise, running down the bleachers to confer with Sarah Kervick at the opening of the rink.

It wasn't the same thing we did in baseball. Our baseball strategy was about Sarah meeting the ball. Now she was applying what I taught her about physics to what she felt when she skated.

"You're not getting enough momentum on that inside Mohawk because you're waiting too long to change feet," I would tell her. "As soon as your shoulders have turned as far as they can go, you need to reverse them and change your feet at the same time. If you wait too long, you'll lose momentum."

I demonstrated from the safety of the rubber matting: "You're making the T shape, you're bringing your free leg up along the skating foot, you're turning your upper body . . . now! Reverse from top to bottom in one motion."

After a few more practice sessions, Sarah would achieve what I'd shown her. It was a funny thing. Unlike in school, Sarah had no problem listening to lectures about skating. She kept her head down and twirled a piece of her hair, concentrating intensely. Then, more often than not, she'd hand me a piece of her clothing and head back to the rink.

The girls began practice in tights, skirts or warm-up pants, sweaters, gloves, hats, and jackets. But all during the practice, they peeled away layer after layer of clothing until they were down to little more than a sleeveless shirt and a skirt. Sarah Kervick had not minded wearing a skirt in the early months. My guess was she would have worn a bodysuit woven of horsehair and nettles as long as they let her on the ice.

No, her decision to stop wearing skating skirts had come about six weeks ago. She'd shown up for practice in baggy warm-up pants, and nothing my mother could say would convince her to go above the ankle. This wasn't merely a fashion whim. Sarah was going against one of Debbi's rules of professionalism. The girls Debbi coached—the girls who were serious about skating—wore skirts, not yoga pants, not warm-ups, *definitely* not jeans. There was a long conference between

Debbi and Sarah in the locker room. When they emerged, Sarah took to the ice again . . . in her pants. It appeared, for the time being anyway, that Sarah had won.

But won what? There was nothing Sarah Kervick wanted more than to skate. Practice, exhibition, competition, she didn't care. Just put her on the ice. She knew what skaters wore when she got into this business.

And I knew her well enough to know she was hiding something. I wanted to ask her about it, but I didn't know how. The laws of mathematics and physics are consistent and logical. Girls, I have found, are neither.

And they don't grow out of it, either. As proof, I will offer up my own mother.

When she dropped us off at Pelican View Elementary after Sarah's practice, she said: "I'm heading back to the rink. I'll pick you up at five-thirty. Oh, and Franklin, I hope you don't mind. I borrowed your dishwashing gloves."

"My dishwashing gloves? For . . . ?"

"Uh . . . washing dishes?"

This was an obvious lie, but she shooed me out of the van before I could interrogate her further.

I sighed. We all had our secrets. *My mother's fascination with the ice rink, Sarah's insistence on wearing pants, my feelings for Glynnis . . .*

"It seems smaller, somehow," Sarah said as we walked to the front entrance.

"And quiet," I added.

School had dismissed an hour earlier, so we entered

through the door by the office. Behind the plate-glass window, we could see Mr. Putnam on the phone. He gave us a cheerful salute. Sarah waved back and we continued down the hall.

"Hey, I've never done this before! Look, Franklin. It's Ms. Linski's room."

"Never done what? Been in the building after school?"

"No. Seen my last year's class. Look, that's where you sat, remember, on the end, so you didn't have germs comin' at you from both sides?"

"Well, that's not exactly the reason I sat there. . . ."

"And I wanted to sit in back, but Ms. Linski made me your partner."

Sarah stared through the window at the empty classroom. Peeking in really did bring back memories. There were Ms. Linski's motivational posters, and her timeline of American history made of cereal-box toys she'd collected on eBay (all carefully sealed in plastic to protect their value). And the wall-mounted hand-sanitizer dispensing unit inspired by yours truly. We cut the incidence of cold and flu outbreaks nearly in half, I might add. And the door to the restroom. I sighed happily, remembering. Yes, every classroom at the elementary school had its own private bathroom.

". . . and you hung your backpack on your chair, and every time you got your calculator or a pencil out of it, you looked over at Glynnis Powell."

"Excuse me?"

"It's pretty obvious you got it goin' on for Glynnis, Franklin."

"Really? How so?"

Sarah managed to pull herself away from Ms. Linski's door. She leaned back against the door jamb.

"Every chance you get, you're moonin' over her. In health class for sure. In the lunchroom. I don't know . . . it's just obvious. Like I-like-skating obvious. Like Mr.-Spansky-spits-on-the-table obvious . . ."

"All right, fine. I understand what you're saying."

We continued down the hall. "It doesn't really matter, now that I know she's a cheerleader. . . ."

"Why?"

"Why? Because cheerleaders hang out with football players, basketball players, soccer players . . . in short, athletes, Sarah, in contact sports. Cheerleaders do not fraternize with QuizBowl finalists and Mathletes."

"How do you know? Did you ask her?"

"Ask her? I can't even get within shouting distance without all my blood rushing to my face."

Sarah shrugged. "Jeez, Franklin, you give up awful easy. . . ."

"That's not true!" I wanted to tell Sarah that if she measured the amount of time I thought about winning Glynnis, the girl would be neck and neck with Franklin Delano Roosevelt, the length of my arms and legs, and keeping my hands clean.

"I wouldn't let anything come between me and skating," Sarah said quietly. "Nothing. You hear that, Franklin?"

This last line sounded faintly aggressive. As if I would suggest such a thing.

"Well, excuse me for confiding," I said, dragging my steps so that Sarah could be the first to reach Mrs. Boardman.

"I could maybe help, you know . . . with you talkin' to Glynnis."

"Thank you . . . ," I said slowly, imagining possible Sarah Kervick techniques for getting up close and personal. "But I already have a plan."

"You do? What is it?"

I explained to her that I intended to gradually spend more time in the vicinity of Glynnis, with the goal at the end of three weeks of waving to her without turning red in the face.

"Jeez . . . at that rate, you'll be a geezer before you get a kiss."

I thought about telling Sarah that love takes time, but then, what did I know about it?

"Have my two helpers arrived to rescue me from this pile of unshelved books?" came a little-old-lady voice from around the corner.

Sarah took off. "Grace!"

"Sarah . . . and Franklin." They stood together as I came into the room, Mrs. Boardman's two hands pressed around Sarah's one. "We'll have to catch up as we work, dears. I'm afraid I am behind my time. Franklin . . ."

Mrs. Boardman gave me a crinkly old-lady smile. "I saved the folktales for you."

I am very familiar with the Dewey decimal system and therefore did not need much direction. I managed to reshelve my entire stack, from the Grimm brothers to stories from *1001*

*Arabian Nights,* while Mrs. Boardman and Sarah worked side by side in nonfiction.

"Oh dear, *Extreme Bicycle Maneuvers,*" Mrs. Boardman chuckled, inserting her ruler between two books on the top shelf. Sarah Kervick pressed the book into place. "What will they think up next? Here's *Surfing in CyberSpace.* That would be right . . . here, I believe."

Sarah fit another book in the space Mrs. Boardman created with her ruler.

"Now, tell me how that lutz is coming. . . ."

Mrs. Boardman had grown up in Norway, where people skated into town down frozen rivers, so she was very interested in Sarah's skating activities. She even knew Debbi, Sarah's skating coach, from church.

"Has Debbi taught you the Scandinavian stop? It was all the rage at the '64 Olympics, you know."

"Not yet, we just do the T and the L so far. She says I shouldn't go too fast."

I agreed with Debbi—when I could understand her Swedish accent—that Sarah should get a complete grounding in fundamentals before she attempted more difficult moves.

After we finished the shelving, Mrs. Boardman gave us a snack: Oreos for Sarah and Tree of Life organic garden vegetable crackers for me.

"And, Franklin, I have some very nice organic lemonade to go along with it."

We sat there, eating over napkins and flipping through our favorite books. It was very peaceful.

Sarah looked up from one of the glossy skating books Mrs. Boardman had ordered for her through interlibrary loan.

"Remember when you used to read to me, Franklin? When you were teaching me?"

I nodded.

She sighed. "We should do that again sometime. You could read that story about Pandora that we got out of the library."

"It was Gloria who said you should read it." Long ago, when I'd hardly known Sarah, Gloria told me to show her the story of Pandora from Greek mythology. It was about a beautiful and curious girl who opens a box and lets all the evil things out into the world: sickness, hate, pain, jealousy, all of it. But she also frees the little winged creature called Hope, who gives heart to all who suffer.

"Well, I've been thinking about that story lately . . . ," Sarah said, drawing her finger across the table, "and I'm wondering this: How does she know where to go? Hope? With all the problems in the world, how does she choose?"

# Filling in the Blanks

That evening, as I sat alone on my bed, tape measure in hand, I made a shocking discovery. My logbook, in which I'd recorded the varying lengths of my arms and legs on their mismatched journey to adulthood, was missing two entries. I had forgotten to measure for two straight days in a row! I needed no one to remind me that those days were gone forever.

Measuring my arms and legs was just a normal part of my day. I'd been doing it for years, ever since I noticed the different rates at which they grew. You see, despite an exhaustive search on the Internet, I had discovered no journal articles devoted to this subject. What if I had a rare and previously undiscovered growth deficiency? Could I be ushering in an age when asymmetrical children struggled with balance? Was all this due to my mother's sinister love of the game "Airplane," in which children are swung around and around by their developing limbs until their predisposition to motion sickness causes them to empty their stomachs?

It was up to me to collect the data. I had three leatherbound journals in which I'd faithfully recorded my measurements over the last five years. The only other entry I'd failed to make was during the influenza outbreak in my ninth year, when I'd been wracked by a 104-degree fever for three days.

I stared at the blank spaces as if they could tell me where I'd gone wrong.

"Franklin!" My mother broke into my thoughts. "I've been calling you for ages. Gloria's on the phone."

Gloria? Calling me? At this hour of the night?

Me: Gloria? This is a surprise.

Gloria: So, how did it work? My advice about the faucets?

Me: Oh. Fine.

Gloria: Good. You know, I was about your age when I got that trick with the faucet from William. Worked every time.

Me: William?

Gloria: My brother, Franklin.

Me: I didn't know you had a brother, Gloria.

Gloria: That's because we rarely stray from your morbid preoccupations. I had four brothers, Franklin. William was the oldest.

Me: You *had* . . .

Gloria: But . . . to the reason I called. Your mother and I have been discussing Sarah, and I wanted your opinion.

Me: Uh, okay.

Gloria: How are things going at school? Is she keeping up? You know, sixth grade is a pivotal year in terms of retention. Students can slip through the cracks when they begin middle school.

Me: Well, her grades aren't what they could be if she just tried—

Gloria: Speak up, Franklin.

Me: She's keeping up, barely, but . . . well . . . I think there is something bothering her. Just today she was asking about that story you told me to read to her last year. She was asking what happened to Hope.

Gloria: Really?

Me: And there's something else going on. At the rink. She won't wear a skirt in practice anymore.

Gloria: I know. Your mother told me. (*big sigh*) I'm going to tell you something personal, Franklin. Is that okay?

Me: Of course, Gloria.

Gloria: I'm thinking about Sarah tonight because she reminds me so much of William. My brother. They shared the same single-minded passion for sport. Only for William, it was football.

Me: Why do you keep talking about him like he's in the past, Gloria? You keep saying *was*.

Gloria: Because William is from the past, Franklin. He died.

Me: Died?

Gloria: Yes. In Vietnam. Today is the anniversary—

Me: He died in Vietnam? Your brother was in combat?

Gloria: It creeps up on me every year. I'd almost forgotten today was the twelfth. . . . (*long, snuffly pause . . . Gloria was blowing her nose.*) All right, then. The security people are shooing me out. Can't work late these days. So you'll watch over Sarah for me?

Me: Sure, Gloria. (*though I was not at all sure what this entailed*)

Gloria: Because she has to skate, Franklin. It's her passion.

When William didn't get a football scholarship, he seemed to lose all hope. And we can't let that happen to Sarah.

Me: Gloria?

Gloria: Yes, Franklin?

Me: I'm sorry about your brother . . . about William.

Gloria: I thought you might understand what I was feeling tonight, Franklin. Every once in a while, you stretch out and touch the world. It gives me hope. (*another long Gloria sigh*) Well, let's call it a day, shall we? My voice gets a little hoarse when I put in so many hours. Don't forget, Franklin, I'm expecting pictures of the big day. A video would be even better. I know you won't let me down.

Me: Bernie's bringing his camera.

Gloria: As for Sarah, she needs you more than ever. As I said, this could be a critical year. I don't like to think of it, but Sarah could be in danger.

Me: Sarah . . . in danger?

Gloria: Yes. Good night, Franklin.

Me: Gloria . . .

I was about to ask her to specify the danger when she disconnected. Certainly, I wanted to ask her how in the world a girl like Sarah Kervick could be in danger when she didn't even acknowledge that such a thing existed. But then I was distracted by thoughts of William. My own experiences of war were limited to old newsreels on the History Channel and the novels from the Accelerated Reader lists I'd gleaned off the Internet, like *All Quiet on the Western Front* and *For Whom the Bell Tolls*.

It was when I started to comb these books for the database

Bernie and I had created on characters most likely to die in preventable accidents that I realized just how dangerous—statistically—it is to be a character in a book. Characters in books are more likely to be injured or killed or just plain die at a far greater rate than the general population.

I should have gone to bed directly, for it was a full twenty minutes past my bedtime. But as I was laying out my clothes for the following morning, I thought about what FDR said during the Second World War: "As a nation, we may take pride in the fact that we are soft-hearted, but we cannot afford to be soft-headed."

Was that why Gloria was working late on such a sad night? Shouldn't she be surrounded by brothers, going through scrapbooks and dabbing at her eyes? Who was comforting her now? If I knew Gloria, she was going home to microwave a Healthy Choice (probably Cajun shrimp), watch the news, and read work-related papers in bed. How would that ease her feelings of sadness?

I went over to my computer and put "William Nelots" into my search engine. I was surprised to find it was quite a common name. I added today's date and found my way to a Web site called thewall-usa.com. I'd stumbled onto a Web site for the Vietnam Veterans Memorial, which listed the soldiers—more than fifty-eight thousand of them—who died in the war. Because the number was so large, soldiers were featured only if it was the anniversary of the day they died, or their birthday.

William Nelots was a single Marine Corps regular from Roanoke, Virginia. He arrived in Vietnam on April 10, 1967, on a nine-month tour of duty. He died two weeks before his twentieth birthday in Quang Nam, South Vietnam, in a hostile conflict using guns and small-arms fire. His body was recovered. He was Protestant.

Statistics have never felt so cold.

At the bottom of the page, there was a button labeled PERSONAL COMMENTS. I clicked on it and discovered several messages had been posted since the Web site went online in 2002.

"I met Willie in September '68 in Okinawa. Willie, or 'Judge,' as we called him, had been with the unit in Khe Sanh, so he tended to take us 'new guys' under his wing and help us get ready for what was to come. Him and another vet stopped me from writing to Mom about how helpless and scared I felt on the eve of our first operation. Judge said, 'They don't need to hear that back home.' "—Manny Singleton, Langley, Washington

"Here's to you, Judge. It's a bit belated but I want to thank you. You have been missed probably more than you ever expected."—fellow marine Rex Trammer, Two Rivers, Wisconsin

"As a vet, I visit the Wall each day through this Web site. If you are here, it is because you have loved and lost. I am always very gratified to see that a man who made the ultimate sacrifice lives on in the memories of his loved ones. God bless Willie and those who served with him."—Robert Roth, Bountiful, Utah

All sorts of people put comments on William "Judge" Nelots' personal-comments page. Some didn't even know him. There were notes from his fellow marines, his football buddies, and his family. I scrolled through the pages until I saw this:

"William, I never called you different. Your shoes were too big. In fact, growing up I swore your feet were on the ground even as your hand was being kissed by the angel Gabriel. I am bitten by sadness every day I wake up and realize my big brother isn't here to take care of me anymore. Langston said it best in 'Poem':

> *I loved my friend.*
> *He went away from me.*
> *There's nothing more to say.*
> *The poem ends,*
> *Soft as it began—*
> *I loved my friend.*

"Rest easy, William. You were a true hero, not just in 'Nam but for Mama, Duane, Paul, David, and me every day you walked this earth. Love, your dearest little Go Go."

*Go Go?*

I went to bed thinking about all the parts of Gloria that I had never known.

# CHAPTER SEVEN

# Feeling Faint at Fiona's Fashions

The following morning, I observed that Miss Mathews' ruffled lavender blouse was missing a button. I did my best *not* to focus on the mole on her collarbone and took my assigned seat next to Sarah Kervick. She appeared to be getting a few extra winks, her head on her desk, her eyes closed.

Miss Mathews cleared her throat to gain the attention of the class. As she began to speak, I noticed one of Mr. Herman's dollies—loaded with a stack of cardboard boxes—up against the whiteboard.

"Due to an unfortunate infestation of miller moths in the kitchen, I was asked this morning to rearrange our health units." At this point, Miss Mathews paged furiously through her class notebook, raising it up until her face was hidden from view. "Adolescent attraction and sexual reproduction will now follow teen pregnancy."

"Hey, isn't that backward?" Tommy Williams asked.

Miss Mathews lowered her notebook to reveal a face that was, well, slightly flushed. Could it be that even college graduates fell victim to undesired social attention? Ignoring Tommy's comment, our teacher produced a dagger-shaped letter opener and sliced through the tape on the topmost box. With admirable speed, Miss Mathews piled its contents on the top of her desk.

Marvin Howerton was the only member of our health class willing to give voice to what we saw in front of us.

"Flour?"

They did indeed appear to be five-pound sacks of Gold Medal flour.

"I'm afraid I . . . I haven't had time to review this lesson," Miss Mathews told us. "So I will have to read from Mr. Teegarten's notes."

Mr. Teegarten, we learned at the beginning of the year, had taken an unexpected early retirement last fall after breaking his nose in a tumble down the bleachers at the big football game between Pelican View and our archrivals, Wing Rock Middle.

"You will work in pairs. I've got the list right here. . . ." As Miss Mathews sifted through the papers on her desk, I wondered if her embarrassment had more to do with being unprepared than with the subject matter we were discussing. Clearly, these arrangements had just been made this morning. She probably had a whole lesson plan carefully prepared on "first crushes," a subject that definitely held my interest, and then arrived at school only to find many kilos of flour stacked in her room, and a sticky note from Mr. London, our assistant principal in charge of curriculum.

"To make it easy, I just used the seating chart, so Joseph-Howerton, Frost-Mirandette, Grandolt-Sprool, Powell-Williams . . ." Unable to locate her list of partners, Miss Mathews was simply pointing pronged fingers at the students as she went up and down the rows. It was gratifying to see that Marvin Howerton had been paired with Brenda Joseph, the only girl to make the Pelican View Middle Boys' Hockey Team. Ha!

I knew long before she got to us that Sarah Kervick would be my partner. Glancing at the sack of flour that now lay between us, I determined that, for the sake of the child, it would probably be best if I was granted full physical custody.

I swiveled in my seat to see how Glynnis would react to being paired with Tommy Williams. She sat upright, looking modestly at the floor, as he reached forward and grabbed his sack of flour, swinging it the way an orangutan might carry a bunch of bananas.

"Look here," he said. "It's the Gingerbread Boy."

"Franklin!" Sarah tugged on my arm. "I don't get it."

"You and I will share this sack of flour and treat it like a baby," I replied, waving the form that was being passed around. "We have to keep track of when we feed it, when we put it down for a nap. . . . Basically," I continued, scanning the assignment, "we have to keep it with us at all times for two weeks."

"You gotta be kidding me. I got cousins that don't get this kind of treatment."

"It's supposed to teach us how hard it is to be a parent so we . . . you know . . . think twice," I answered her in a low voice.

Sarah Kervick processed what I said for just a moment before making a sour face.

"I feel the very same way about you," I informed her, taking one from a stack of oversized paper lunch bags being handed around.

"You need to think of this as a real baby," Miss Mathews read from her notebook, "so draw a face on the bag and slip the flour inside it. Remember to keep it with you at all times. No, you may not set it down to jiggle the handle on your locker. If you wouldn't do it to a real infant, then you can't do it to your flour baby.

"You'll have to have one of your parents review your log at the end of the day and give your baby a 'well check.' They have to initial each daily log. I've got the forms here."

Sarah Kervick was tapping her pencil on the top of the desk in a most annoying manner.

"Why don't you think up a name?" I suggested, handing her the "birth certificate." "I'll handle the face."

Her hand shot up.

"Yes, Sarah?"

"What if you know you're not gonna have any kids? Ever. Do you still have to do it?"

"But you can't know that, Sarah. You're too young."

Sarah folded her arms and sunk down in her seat so that her nose was level with the writing surface. "If I said I'm not gonna have any," she muttered, "I'm not gonna have any."

"Well, if it helps, I believe you," I told her. Sarah Kervick belonged with a gym bag, not a diaper bag.

"Franklin, I mean it." Sarah sat up and grabbed my shoulder and shook it. It hurt! "I'm supposed to take this sack of flour home and tell my dad it's a *baby*? And have him check on it? He'll laugh me right out of the trailer!"

"Sarah, what is the matter?" I asked, trying not to cringe from the pain of her tightening grip. She let go and sat back down at her desk. As I watched her tap manically on her desktop, it occurred to me that something really was very wrong with her circuitry. Normally, she would just shrug her shoulders and do a haphazard job of the assignment. Why was she taking things so seriously all of a sudden?

I tried again. "Sarah?"

"Not now," she whispered, grabbing the handout I passed to her and turning as far away from me as her desk would allow.

I tried to focus on the assignment and compose a reasonable facsimile of a human baby onto a paper bag with my #2 pencil. All this emotional upheaval with Sarah Kervick was drawing attention away from the real tragedy that had occurred in Room 401B that morning. Glynnis Powell was carrying another man's sack of flour. Yes, the object of my affection was working out feeding schedules with a boy whose only claim to fame was making fart noises with his armpits.

Between sketching baby eyebrows, I stole glances at Glynnis as she took a straight edge from her pencil case and began to make a chart. Carefully, she placed the metal edge on her paper, biting her lip in concentration.

Sarah Kervick was absorbed in her shoes. I glanced over at the "birth certificate" she was supposed to be filling out. Only one item was complete. Next to Baby's First Name, Sarah had written "Keds." She sat there, her head in her hands, staring at her own handwriting.

She was upset. Some sort of response was called for on my part. What would William have done if this were "Go Go"? I put my hand on Sarah's forearm.

"Are you okay?"

Sarah pressed the heels of both her hands into her eyes. When she looked up at me, they were wet with tears.

"I haven't seen my dad for the last two nights."

She followed this up by declaring through gritted teeth, "And if you *ever* tell anyone what I just told you, I'll tie your arms in a knot and throw you in the Grand River."

"Where exactly are we going again?" I asked after school as my mother hustled me and Sarah into her work van.

"Her name is Fiona Foster, and the guys down at the rink say she makes the best dresses." She looked over her shoulder and gazed meaningfully at Sarah in the backseat.

"Did you say 'Foster'?" I asked. Was it possible we were about to visit the home of Rebecca Foster? Had she been referring to this meeting when she said Donuthead was on her calendar?

"You might want to prepare yourself mentally, Sarah," my mother continued. "She's going to measure you."

"What for?"

I lowered my voice and turned to Sarah. "Can we just get this over with as quickly as possible? For my sake?"

Sarah looked at me. "You're not supposed to let strangers touch you," she said quietly.

Despite hours of listening to classic rock at dangerously high volume, my mother has excellent hearing.

"Fiona Foster is a seamstress, not a stranger. She's had her hands on practically every girl at the skating rink and they survived. Come on, Sarah."

But Sarah didn't answer. She sat, hunched and silent, staring out the window. The tears from the morning were long gone, but the way she kept her lips pressed together and swallowed hard every so often made me realize they could come back. Anyone else staring at her at that moment might think she was mad as the dickens. But I knew a thing or two about Sarah Kervick.

I also knew a thing or two about my mother. Sarah's stubbornness about this dress was getting on her last nerve. I sent a mental suggestion to Sarah to *tell my mother what's going on*. Not that I had a complete picture myself. The dress was the least of my worries. A girl her age should not be left alone all night. Sarah had made me promise not to tell anyone, so all I could do with the information she'd given me was worry!

Also, I'm not very experienced at keeping secrets. The only other time I'd been asked was when my mother made me promise not to reveal to Rick, her last boyfriend, that she'd ordered prescription-strength Skintactix, the most popular adult acne medication, on the Home Shopping Network. As we sat in the van in silence, I tried to think of something—anything—to say besides *Sarah's father has disappeared!*

We parked next to a split-level with a sign out front that announced FIONA'S FASHIONS. My mother turned around in her seat. "Help us out here, Franklin," she said.

As I may have mentioned, shopping under any circumstances is not my mother's strong suit. I opened the van door for Sarah. Together, our mood could only be described as somber.

But Fiona Foster, who threw wide the door to her "lower-level fashion studio," was determined to outcompete our gloom with her enthusiasm.

"Skaters!" she said, waving her free arm in a dramatic curlicue. "You are most welcome."

Fiona Foster was, to quote my mother, "a piece of work." She looked a bit like a Barbie doll that has spent too much time in the sun.

So *this* was Rebecca Foster's gene pool.

My mother followed Fiona Foster down the stairs into the darkened basement.

I grabbed Sarah's arm. "Shouldn't we do something? I mean, about your dad. Maybe call the police?"

Sarah looked at me. She seemed disgusted by the suggestion. "Do something? Do what? He's done it before, Franklin. Just drop it, okay? He'll be back." She let out a long sigh through her nose, and headed down.

I took a deep breath and followed her. In a clatter of steps, we entered a dimly lit room filled with that suffocating moldy-basement smell. Fiona plunged farther into the darkness.

"I want to turn on the lights all at once so you get the full effect," she said. "We just finished the remodel. Ta da!"

The "remodel" seemed to consist of stringing white Christmas lights around the drop ceiling. Surely, the pink shag carpet could not be new since it was already stained in several places. A tall metal cabinet stood along the far wall next to a floor mirror, and a shower rod with a plastic floral curtain was rigged up over a corner of the room.

Sarah, my mother, and I lined up against the wall as Fiona

rushed back toward us. We'd been herded into an alcove next to a wrought-iron café table piled with big books of skating costumes.

Between Sarah's home life and Fiona's home, my senses were so overloaded that I sank into one of the wrought-iron chairs against the wall without examining the seat first. As if on cue, a long-haired cat leapt into my lap and began to purr furiously, releasing clouds of hair and dander all over my carefully maintained khakis.

"Uh," I said to Fiona's mass of blond hair, for that was all we could see of her as she extracted ice cube trays from a mini fridge under the utility sink.

"Oh, that's Chester," she said, straightening. "He loves everybody. Anyone for a refreshing glass of Crystal Light?"

We shook our heads no. My mother sat down on the other side of the table and heaved a skating book onto her lap.

"Well, then," Fiona said cheerfully, dropping the tray onto the plywood that spanned the utility sink, "you must be Sarah." She picked up a pink clipboard and wound a measuring tape around her neck like a scarf.

Sarah nodded and looked at the floor.

Fiona began to read. "According to Julia here, you're entered in the junior division of the GPVAFSA's regional tournament, but that's in"—here she paused to spread her fingers flat across her bony chest—"a little over two weeks . . . with the exhibition in"—more dramatic clutching—"a week and a half?

"You gals must think I'm a miracle worker."

There was a long pause that we filled by examining the pile on the shag carpet. Not a one of us favored the term "gal."

"*But . . .* I do have a secret weapon."

Fiona trotted over to her metal cabinet and yanked open the doors. The rusted grating of its hinges startled Chester, who released another handful of hair into the atmosphere before digging his claws into my thighs and leaping.

I cried out, which seemed like the appropriate response to being impaled by a dozen needle-sharp objects. My mother took no action other than a quick glance in my direction, leaving me to sift through drifts of hair to search for puncture wounds on my own.

Sarah Kervick had withdrawn into herself. One glance at her face was enough to confirm she wasn't daydreaming. But she wasn't with us in the room, either. It took several seconds of disregarding my own pain and discomfort to realize that I had never seen this look before. It wasn't bored (reserved for school), blissful (reserved for skating), hero-worshiping (reserved for my mother), or disgusted, impatient, or frustrated (all reserved for me). No. Sarah Kervick looked sad. Very sad. How could I know that the look on her face would unsettle me even more than the filthy feline lumbering toward a litter box with a funny hitch in his gait?

I wasn't sure which made me more uncomfortable. I began plotting our escape.

"Okay, so what kind of show are you doing? What's the theme?" Fiona asked, searching through the dresses that were hanging in the cabinet.

"I keep these in stock for emergencies," she explained. "There are a dozen different styles here: jazz, country and western, waltz, classical . . . we need to match your costume to your music."

My mother looked at Sarah, waiting for her to engage. Sarah looked at the floor. My mother looked at me.

It was a simple enough question. "She's skating to the second half of Ravel's *Bolero*," I informed Fiona, trying to move things along.

"Aah . . . Spanish." Fiona cupped her chin in one thin hand, yanked a dress off the rack, and held it up. "It's basic black for *Bolero*, with maybe some red accents. We can modify a ready-made."

She held the dress out, her eyes flicking from it to Sarah's chest.

Sarah glanced up at the dress. "Yeah, that's good," she mumbled.

"Sarah," my mother said. "You haven't even tried it on yet."

Fiona hung the dress back in the cabinet and unwound the measuring tape from around her neck. She advanced toward Sarah.

I closed my eyes, picturing a personal-assault lawsuit involving my family name.

"Come on, Sarah. I'll help." My mother stood up and put her hand on Sarah's shoulder. "Can I?" she asked Fiona as she held out her hand for the tape measure.

"Well, I guess so," Fiona said, though clearly she saw this sort of activity as belonging to her. "She has to stand completely still. Moving around corrupts the numbers."

As my mother's hand closed around the tape measure, Sarah took a step back.

"The most important measure is the torso," Fiona said,

grabbing her clipboard and closing in. "Put the tape on the right shoulder, loop it between the legs, and return."

My mother looked at Fiona as if she'd just instructed her to run the measuring tape between the legs of a Bengal tiger.

Sarah crossed her arms over her chest. "I changed my mind," she said.

"I'm sorry . . . you what?"

At this exact moment of high tension, a cloud of red-and-white Pelican View Panther came plummeting down the steps.

"Ma, I gotta be back at school by three-thirty. . . ."

I knew that voice. I tried to cover my face with my hands, hoping to avoid a scene more unpleasant than this one already was, but Chester's hair still clung to my fingers . . . disgusting!

"Rebecca!" barked Fiona. "It's business. What did I tell you . . . ?"

"It's not you . . . it's just . . ." Sarah's voice had risen to the point where *she* now earned our attention. She was speaking to my mother, the expression on her face having descended from sad to miserable.

"You have to know it! One of these days . . . *real soon,* I'm gonna look up and you'll be gone. . . ." Her voice trailed off as she turned away from my mother. "And I can't . . ."

Sarah flung out her arm as if to take it all in: the sample dresses, Fiona chewing her thumbnail, the table piled high with skating catalogs. "I can't do all this by myself."

Everyone froze. Somehow, even Rebecca understood that what was going on at the other end of the room trumped the drama of whether or not she would be late for the game bus.

My mother was stunned. "Sarah," she said. The tape measure dropped to the floor. "Why would you say that?"

"Because it happens every time," Sarah said quietly, her eyes locked on the cement wall over my mother's shoulder. "Even you can't change it."

My mother took a step back, waiting I assume, for Sarah to explain just what she meant by "it." She was trying to figure out what just happened. I wasn't sure myself, but I think Sarah wanted us to tell her that whatever she was sure would happen wasn't going to. I think Sarah Kervick wanted to be reassured.

"I know you!" Rebecca had snapped out of her stunned silence. "And you." She pointed at Sarah.

"You two are supposed to do the presentation in health class on How to Tell If It's Really Love."

Without considering how this would affect things with Glynnis, or even how my words might correlate with future violent acts perpetrated on me by football players who would defend Rebecca's honor, I said to her: "And I know you, Ms. Foster. Your face is in the dictionary next to the word *cretin*."

"Huh?"

I thought as much.

My mother had pulled her wallet out of her back pocket. She handed a credit card to Fiona.

"I'll be in the car," she said.

Fiona glanced around helplessly. "But don't you have a preference? Mothers always have a preference! Should I add pleats? A handkerchief hem? For a little extra, I could do rhinestone accents."

"But I'm not the mother, am I?" Though she was answering Fiona, my mother was looking directly at Sarah. "Come on, Franklin."

I, too, looked at Sarah. Her eyes were fixed on the floor. She seemed to have collapsed standing up. She looked so utterly sad that I almost begged my mother to make up and finish the job.

But then a most vile smell reached my nostrils, and I observed Chester exiting the litter box and advancing toward me, shaking out his hind legs.

And I fled.

As I hustled past Rebecca, she stuck out her tongue.

In an extremely thoughtless grade-school gesture, I stuck out mine, too.

"Really?" Fiona was waving her clipboard, agitated. She followed us up the stairs and into the gloriously fresh outdoor air. "No preference for sleeve length? Maybe a jewel neckline? Beads? Red? Black?"

"Whatever you said," my mother replied, without turning around. "Make it go with her music."

We sat in the van for exactly eleven minutes in complete silence. My mother didn't even turn on the radio or chew gum. I tried to distract myself by finding additional safety and health violations in the Fosters' yard: an upended rake, a roller skate in the driveway, an unsecured, industrial-sized bag of Trevor-Time cat food (regularly hawked on the cable-access channel by pet expert Trevor Thompson).

But I was unable to get the expression on Sarah Kervick's face out of my mind.

Why? What did her crazy comment or her body language or her miserable expression have to do with the tenets set forth by our thirty-second president of health promotion, risk avoidance, and mental improvement? Had FDR overlooked something? Was a tenet missing?

I resolved to check out my new tome on adolescence, *What's Going On Down There,* to see if this new concern for others was related to a surge in my hormones. Through the passenger-side window, I watched Sarah walk slowly up to the van and get in. My mother studied her fingers before starting the engine. I took the credit card Sarah passed to the front seat.

Fiona came up the steps in a rush and launched herself toward the van, her high heels piercing the lawn, her hands clamped around a ring of keys. Rebecca followed her. She looked toward the van and shook her fist at me before hopping into a late-model Ford Taurus with a dangling tailpipe.

Fiona rapped on the driver-side window. "You're sure about this? It's highly unusual," she said, squeezing the fuzzy dice on her key chain.

My mother cracked the window. "Does it go with her show?"

To my horror, Fiona put a key in her mouth and sucked on it, thinking.

"Yes, but it's nothing I've ever—"

"Then you did your job. When can we pick it up?"

"How about Monday? After four? I work out on Monday, is all. Helps with the stress."

The last few words I had to lip-read as my mother chose to drive away midsentence.

# Positive Electricity

My mother is nothing if not stubborn. She said "a sandwich after" and that meant "a sandwich after," even if the three people now sitting in a booth at Perkins' Drug Store, the combination pharmacy and sandwich shop with the real soda fountain dating back to 1955, had no appetite whatsoever.

I tried to be chipper. "Maybe I'll try the taco salad," I said, "without taco meat, of course."

"That's an expensive way to get lettuce and tomatoes."

"And cheese," I added. "I don't think I've achieved my USDA-recommended amount of calcium today."

Sarah sat across from us, looking at the menu. "I'm not very hungry."

She glanced over at my mother, obviously longing for something that was not on the menu.

"Just order what you usually get," my mother said. "You can eat it later."

It was clear to me that they both felt bad about what had happened, but "feelings" were not a specialty of Sarah Kervick or my mother. I might have attempted to at least pull them to the center of the ring to shake hands, but the waitress—otherwise known as Mrs. Perkins—approached our table.

"Julia, Franklin, Sarah . . . hello, dear." She slid in next to Sarah and put her arm around her. "Julia's been telling us all about your big day."

There was something about Mrs. Perkins that let her get away with touching people. She had that rosy-cheeked, Mrs. Santa Claus look, and she always smelled like cinnamon rolls, which—though I avoided them like the plague due to their high fat content—did give off a very nice aroma.

"Why so glum, everyone? Bad day at school?"

This completely reasonable question was met with another silence.

Instead of pressing the issue, Mrs. Perkins stood up, slapped her apron, and said: "I'm just going to have to make you all a chocolate shake. And Sarah, I'm putting a couple of eggs in yours. When Davy was in training for the Pelican View AAU Swim Team, I used to give him a shake with a couple of raw eggs in it every evening. All that extra protein shaved two full seconds off his hundred-meter backstroke."

I was about to acquaint Mrs. Perkins with a deadly little germ that lurked in raw eggs called "salmonella" when I happened to glimpse a familiar pair of legs pressed up against the makeup counter.

"I need the Vermilion Sunset, both the lipstick and the nail polish."

There, in a pair of spandex shorts and a GET THE PI PHI HIGH T-shirt, was none other than my sixth-grade health teacher, Miss Mathews, looking to all the world like a college co-ed on spring break, and ordering *lipstick* from a smiling Mr. Perkins.

Mr. Perkins set two enormous grocery bags on the counter. "Those on the EMS account, too?" he asked.

"Well, I *am* their number one volunteer," Miss Mathews replied, "but I don't think the county's emergency medical service is willing to buy my lipstick ration, do you, Mr. Perkins?"

I couldn't believe my ears. Miss Mathews was flirting! With a married man.

"Franklin, dear? Are you all right?" Mrs. Perkins reached over and pressed the back of her hand to my forehead. "You don't have a fever," she said, frowning.

"It's the egg thing," my mother presumed. "You know, raw."

"Oh . . . I suppose you're right. Egg Beaters then. That will do the trick."

I tried to get Sarah Kervick's attention, using my eyebrows to indicate the direction her gaze should take. She glanced up at me and shrugged, obviously not willing to take the time to see what I'd discovered.

Having completed her purchase, Miss Mathews struggled past us, carrying her bags full of medical supplies for the EMS. But then, like everybody else, she had to stop to say hello to Mrs. Perkins. I was sinking lower into the booth, my hands on the edge of the table for balance, when she spotted me.

"Franklin? Sarah? So you two really are friends."

Mrs. Perkins performed the introductions, using Miss Mathews' first name.

"Hey, Elaine," my mother said before returning to study her menu. I felt the urge to give her a poke to make her sit up straight and be pleasant.

But my mother was clearly not in the mood to be social.

"Did you know Sarah's a figure skater, Elaine?" Mrs. Perkins said into the awkward silence. "She's quite talented, I hear."

Miss Mathews balanced her bags on the back of the booth and looked at Sarah Kervick with interest. "I love to watch skating on TV. Not much chance of me being a skater, though, growing up in Arizona." She made a little snort through her nose.

"Can I come watch you sometime?"

Sarah tilted her head to look up at Miss Mathews.

"You can come to the exhibition with Mr. Perkins and me," Mrs. Perkins said, putting her hand on Miss Mathews' arm. "Sarah's going to have a whole section of cheerleaders."

*First raw eggs in the milk shake. Then Miss Mathews in spandex, and now the mention of cheerleaders?!*

"Franklin, there you go with that look again. He might need a couple of cold cucumbers and some time on the sofa when you get home, Julia."

Sarah reached across the table and tugged on my mother's sleeve. "I have to tell you something," she said, casting a long cool glance at the rest of us. "In private."

My mother looked at her over the top of the menu.

"Well, I'll get started on that shake." Mrs. Perkins brushed off the front of her apron, even though there was nothing there.

Miss Mathews sighed and picked up her bags. "I need to get going as well."

Can you say *Get lost* with your eyebrows? My mother was making every attempt as she stared at me.

I refolded my napkin.

I felt a surge of hope that Sarah would share the details of her missing father with my mother, which would then take the burden off me for knowing that she was being left alone—all night!—with nothing but a couple of wild dogs to look after her.

"Maybe I could . . . that is, Miss Mathews, do you need some help with your bags?"

"What a gentleman, Franklin," my mother said enthusiastically.

"That is so sweet," Miss Mathews said. "I had to park a few blocks away." She heaved a sack into my hands before I'd replaced my napkin on the table. Before I knew it, I was walking down Main Street side by side with our health teacher. In her athletic attire!

"My car is just down by the post office," Miss Mathews said from behind her bag.

I glanced into mine and saw roles of adhesive tape, Ace bandages, rubbing alcohol. I tried to formulate a polite question about emergency medical needs, but I felt much more comfortable pushing my face into the brown paper bag.

Miss Mathews was chatting away happily. I suppose, like most of her students, her mood lifted considerably after school, too.

"Next, I go to the grocery store. After doing this for two years, I feel like I'm shopping for my own family. Len Spansky eats only shaved-tavern-ham-and-horseradish-mustard sandwiches, and Pearl is a vegetarian. I have to go to Harvest Health to get the ingredients for her tempeh Reubens. . . ."

"Mr. Spansky's in the EMS?" I blurted out, thinking of the unfortunate accident victims over whose wounds our science teacher hovered. Did he bring his spray bottle to the EMS?

"Oh no, not our science teacher. He's Arthur. I'm talking about his brother, Leonard. Here we are." Miss Mathews pointed to a very small convertible, the kind they advertised as "sporty." My mind reeled with the possibilities for tragic accidents in this vehicle.

After she tossed both our bags into the backseat, Miss Mathews put her hand on my shoulder. I tried to exhibit excellent posture and look Miss Mathews in the eye as Emily Post recommends, but unfortunately, I had to confine my gaze to her pink athletic shoes.

"Your mother is right, Franklin. You are quite a gentleman," Miss Mathews said, squeezing. It wasn't a Sarah Kervick squeeze, I can tell you that. It sent pleasant little prickles of electricity down the short side of my body.

"Well," she said, opening the door and sinking into the seat of her sports car, "off to D & W to get the groceries." She pulled a kerchief out of her glove compartment and tied it over her head. Not like Glynnis, who tied hers at the back underneath her hair. No, Miss Mathews tied hers beneath her chin.

As if she knew what I was thinking, she said: "Keeps my hair from whipping around."

Then, with lightning speed and very little concern for oncoming traffic, Miss Mathews reversed out of her tight spot and sped away, waving one arm all the way to the traffic light.

I took several deep breaths to allow my blood flow to return to its normal route and went back to Perkins' Drug Store. Through the window, I saw Sarah and my mother deep in conversation. The food had been delivered. My plate of lettuce garnished with tomatoes and cheese did not look very appetizing.

"Franklin," my mother said when I returned, "we couldn't wait. We were starving. How long does it take to help someone to their car?" She cast a sideways glance at Sarah. "Maybe Miss Mathews takes a little longer." Sarah's mouth was full, so she pressed the back of her hand against it to keep in the food while she laughed.

"If you're trying to cover up for the fact that you've started eating without me, it's not working," I told my mother, before excusing myself to use the facilities.

"Don't be sore, Franklin," Sarah said as I rounded the corner. "We got you the no-salt chips."

At least Sarah seemed in better spirits, I thought, as I hummed my way through three leisurely verses.

But she'd told my mother nothing. For we dropped Sarah off at her house as usual, and my mother acted like this was just an ordinary day.

"I wonder where her dad is," I mused, looking out the window as we drove away.

"He's working late this week. Sarah told me."

I bet she did.

What, then, should I do? I was sworn to secrecy. I wanted to confide in someone, but who? Gloria? After a restless night, I resolved to call her before school and casually ask about the legality of leaving minors unattended. Not for the day, but for days! Two to be exact. Maybe even three. But when I called her at approximately 6:40 a.m. eastern standard time, I got her message machine. Ever since Gloria installed caller ID, I noticed that her machine picked up a lot more often, especially in the morning.

There was nothing left to do but go to school. I distracted myself by thinking about Glynnis. Even before seven, the thought of her hair pulled into a neat ponytail, and the starched collar that encircled her neck, gave me hope that my world might someday return to its previously tidy and ordered state.

At 6:57 a.m., I rang Bernie's doorbell. Mrs. Lepner opened the door. She was wearing her chenille bathrobe and had not yet brushed her teeth. I kept the small talk to a minimum as she bundled Bernie into a goose-down coat to ward off the chill morning air. Kissing his forehead, she positioned his shoulders parallel to the door frame and launched him onto the front stoop.

After the slightest pause to ensure the weight of my backpack was evenly distributed, I said: "Bernie, I need to confide in you. A rather delicate matter of the heart."

Now, Bernie Lepner is not what I'd consider an expert in matters of the heart. In fact, the only thing Bernie is well-versed enough in to be considered an expert is *The Encyclopedia of Mythical Beasts*. But he was my friend, and so I felt he should be willing to stretch a little.

"Bernie?" I grabbed the back of his jacket to detour him around a jogger who had stopped to tie his shoe.

"Okay, Franklin."

"You may have noticed that last year I spoke rather enthusiastically about Glynnis Powell. I think I even mused in your presence about what literature she might read. This should give you some indication of the depth of my feelings toward her."

"I like Glynnis, too. She's my tutor."

"Excuse me?"

"My tutor. She helps me with stuff."

"You have regular contact with Glynnis Powell and you never told me?"

"Are you okay, Franklin? You almost stepped into the street on a flashing hand."

It took me a moment to return to myself. Of course. I had yet to confide my tender feelings, so Bernie would have no way of knowing how deeply this information would affect me.

"What sort of *stuff* does she help you with?"

"Oh, I have trouble being organized. I forget to write things down. Sometimes I don't turn in my assignments. Glynnis helps me with all that."

"That's what I do for Sarah, Bernie."

"My mom said that, too. But you complain a lot about it, so I figured you weren't interested. Miss Rhonda set me up with Glynnis. She gets community-service hours for helping me."

We walked along in silence as I digested this. Glynnis and I had even more in common than I realized. I didn't know you could get community-service hours for helping out a fellow student. This tutoring thing made even more sense in my case, as Sarah Kervick's considerable energy might take an anti-social turn were she not continually occupied on the skating rink *or* at our dining-room table inserting chopsticks into my electric pencil sharpener.

Maybe there was an after-school club where fellow do-gooders could relax with serving-sized pouches of organic popcorn and bottles of purified water and discuss the finer points of motivating our peers to academic excellence. Well, proficiency. Maybe, in certain cases, a legally acceptable attendance record and a GPA in the low C range.

"Bernie," I said, unable to meet his gaze. "My feelings toward Glynnis go way beyond friendship. I have"—here I paused to put an ice-cold hand to my burning cheek—"pledged my affections to her and to her alone."

My mind traveled from the ecologically conscious cloth napkins she used in the lunchroom to the sprinkle of freckles across her nose—which could be attributed to her Norse ancestors and certainly not a lack of sensible sun protection.

"Do you think, Bernie, that Glynnis might consider sitting with us at lunch?" I asked in an agony of longing. "Even though she's a cheerleader?"

It was then I realized I'd misinterpreted Bernie's silence.

"Bernie?" I took hold of his shoulders and forced him to look at me.

Bernie worried his hands a bit. "I'm sorry, Franklin. Were you talking to me?"

I sighed, wondering if perhaps my mother might have been a better place to start sharing my feelings about the opposite sex, though a decade of observing her dating habits would indicate otherwise.

"You were saying something about Glynnis," Bernie prodded, trying to care.

"Yes, I was." We were now being sucked toward the mouth of Pelican View Middle, surrounded by hundreds of other adolescents. This hardly seemed the time for a confession of true love. Bernie slowed down and tugged on my sleeve.

"Franklin, I might as well tell you, I'm not going to be in school Monday. My dad has a job interview in Gary and we're going with him to look at schools."

"You're what?"

"I'm going to Gary. Gary, Indiana. And I won't be here Monday."

We were inside now, pressing toward our lockers. I dodged a girl marching straight ahead with a note in her hand. Suddenly, I felt like the Karner blue butterfly, or Kirtland's warbler, both endangered species in our fair state. My small band was only three in number. Sarah Kervick's life was spinning out of control. Bernie was now threatening flight to points south.

I twirled the dials on my locker, completely forgetting my own combination. The numbers didn't return to me until I was clapped on the shoulder by Sarah Kervick.

"You can quit worrying. He's back," she said.

# CHAPTER NINE

# Measuring Up

Okay, I admit it. I don't like being home alone. Especially at night. Especially on a weekend. It doesn't take a rocket scientist to figure out that far more home invasions occur on weekend evenings than weekdays, but do you think the Lions Club takes this into account when they plan their Friday-night combination dance and fish fry, guaranteed to keep parents out beyond ten o'clock? And who decided that eleven-and-three-quarters years old was old enough to "hold down the fort," as my mother says? It made me marvel, once again, at Sarah's bravery. She stayed alone in that trailer for two nights and three days and didn't complain about it.

As soon as I got home from school, I tried to distract myself from the knowledge that I would be alone all evening by reading my latest issue of *Germs and Their Genesis*. This did not prove to be a wise idea. The lead article focused on a study from Sweden that attributes the dramatic rise of pediatric asthma and allergy cases to—of all things—clean households. Dubbed the "hygiene hypothesis," it warns that living in a world with antibacterial hand wash, tissues, and counter wipes is hazardous to your health.

It seems that European farm children have a very low incidence of allergies and asthma, as well as dermatitis, multiple sclerosis, Crohn's disease, and type 1 diabetes. These so-called scientists suggest that ultraclean conditions do not properly prepare one's immune system, leaving kids more vulnerable to allergies involving pollen, dust, peanuts, even their own body tissue in the form of flaky skin. Excuse me???

I forced myself to read on. The solution? Send your children to day care and get some filthy pets. In other words, expose them to all sorts of low-level bacterial dangers to strengthen their immune response. I expect, in some upcoming issue, the Swedes will have me sharing my bedroom with a couple of goats and a potbellied pig!

Sarah Kervick wasn't the only one with overloaded circuits. What was I supposed to do with all this conflicting information? Was I now supposed to shovel in potluck casseroles without dissecting them for dog hair first? Especially my mother's friend Penny's? Should I stop flossing, walk into my bedroom with outdoor shoes, write with pencils that bear Sarah's tooth marks?

To handle this bombshell, I needed to place an immediate phone call to the one person in the United States with the qualifications to address my concerns.

Gloria: *Gwooria Unwots hee.*

Me: Gloria?

Gloria: Sorry, Franklin, you caught me in the middle of my potato salad.

Me: That's all right, Gloria. I'll wait.

Gloria (*still chewing*): I picked up because I need to talk to you.

Me: Really?

Gloria: I've been asked to form a committee to study the relationship between curvature of the spine in adolescent boys and video-game playing. And since I am neither a boy nor a video-game player, I thought maybe you could help.

Me: Well, naturally, I've formed some opinions along those lines. On the whole, video games directed at boys are quite violent, Gloria. . . .

Gloria: I'm not interested in your opinions, Franklin. What I need is information.

Me: Information?

Gloria: Yes, what are boys playing these days? Do they play alone or together? Do they lie on their stomachs, sit cross-legged, use straight-back chairs or upholstered furniture? . . . What was on your mind, by the way?

Me (*I glance down at my notes, ready to launch an attack on the research methods used in the hygiene hypothesis or at least get some statistics on the possibility of a weekend home invasion, but somehow other words come out of my mouth.*): Everything's changing, Gloria. I keep forgetting to measure my arms and legs; my mother seems to have lost all sense, now that she has a boyfriend, and you know, Gloria, she wasn't particularly sensible to begin with. . . . (*My words gain momentum. Everything spills out. Do I really have to give up my antibacterial hand wash? Is it possible that Bernie will move to Gary, Indiana? Sarah Kervick cried, for Pete's sake!*)

Gloria: Everything is not changing, Franklin. You are.

Me: I am? But why should I change?

Gloria: You shouldn't, necessarily. You just are. It's called "growing up," Franklin. You are beginning to notice that other people have needs wholly unconnected to your health; important things happen to them that have nothing to do with you. You are beginning to recognize that they have feelings.

Me: Really?

Gloria: Yes, really. It's a good sign, Franklin. Remember the Roseto Effect?

Me: Of course I do! I was fine until that study came along.

Gloria: Let's review it, shall we? For me?

Me (*heavy sigh*): In some little town called Roseto, Pennsylvania, people were doing everything wrong: smoking and drinking too much, eating lots of fatty foods. . . . But they were living longer than the people in the towns around them. Scientists figured out that it was because they had good friends and family close by. They enjoyed spending time with their loved ones. Come to think of it, they probably had filthy dogs lounging on their couches waiting for them to get home, just like in the hygiene hypothesis!

Gloria: But most important, they felt their lives had meaning, Franklin. You want the same thing. You want your life to have meaning.

Me: But my life *does* have meaning, Gloria.

Gloria (*choking noise*): Sorry, wrong pipe.

Me: Gloria . . . did you change?

Gloria: Of course I changed. I'm an adult now . . . with responsibilities.

Me: But I'm not an adult yet.

Gloria: That may be true, Franklin. But some people age faster than others, and I'm afraid you're one of them.

• • •

I thought about all this as I sat in the hall listening to the conversation coming from my mother's bedroom. What exactly did Gloria mean when she said "Some people age faster"? She disconnected before I could get a thorough explanation. Was she trying to say that one part of me was growing faster than the other, something like the left and right sides of my body? Could my brain be getting bigger at a rate faster than my skull could accommodate? Or was Gloria just being sarcastic, as she has a tendency to be when I ask questions she doesn't want to answer?

"Would you hurry up?" my mother said to Penny. "It's almost five. He's going to be here any minute." Paul was coming extra early so he could show my mother off around town before the dance began.

"I'm a makeup artist. You can't make art on a schedule. Hold still."

I wanted to ask Penny if she'd sterilized the Q-tips she was using to apply makeup to my mother's face, but it was made clear to me that I was to stay out of the room until the artist was finished. It was just my luck that my mother chose a friend who liked applying makeup *and* grooming her three rescued greyhounds.

"Not eye shadow. Really? Do I have to?"

"Listen, when I put this mocha in the crease, your eyes will pop."

"I didn't know the pop-eyed look was in."

"Honestly, Julia, you know what I mean. Now hold still."

The doorbell rang.

"Franklin!"

I answered the door, trying my best to look stern. I didn't want Paul to think he could keep my mother out past midnight just because he'd bought a couple of twenty-five-dollar tickets to a charity affair.

"Paul?" The man standing in front of me wore a navy-blue suit with a light-blue dress shirt and a gray tie. With the hair on his head combed and the dirt under his fingernails scrubbed away, Paul looked almost, well, presentable.

"Franklin, my man. Well, what do you think? I don't get to wear these duds too often." Paul completed a full turn for my benefit. "Seriously, do you like the blue on blue? I was debating."

"The blue on blue looks very nice, Paul, but I think we should talk about what time you'll be bringing my mother home this evening."

"Honestly, Franklin, you're worse than my dad when I was seventeen."

Paul whistled softly through his teeth. My mother was framed in the doorway with the light from the hall shining down on her hair. Her cheeks glowed, her eyes sparkled. She looked like she belonged on television pointing at game-show prizes.

"A pretty girl," Paul sang, sticking the box he'd brought along into my hands, "is like a melody. Come here."

You could see through the plastic top of the Fields' Flowers box. I looked at the flowers Paul had brought as my mother took hold of his lapels.

"Mmmm. You smell good, too." There followed sounds of kissing.

"Didn't I tell you, Pen, she'd look great in a dress?"

"Yeah, yeah. She looks great. But what about her makeup? C'mon. Don't you think this should be Julia's new look? I call it natural sophistication."

"Give it a rest, Penny. Do you have to go on?" my mother said.

"She doesn't need anything. She's perfect the way she is." More kissing. Before I even had a chance to look away! I guess Paul Bernard knew all the lines. I handed my mother the box of flowers to get it over with. My mother is crazy about flowers.

"Paul . . ." She lifted the little bouquet out of the box and clipped it around her wrist. "They match my dress perfectly. How did you know?"

Paul winked at Penny. "I did a little snooping." He took my mother's arm and folded it across her chest, admiring the match. "They look pretty good, don't they?" Paul waited for Penny and me to agree enthusiastically before continuing. "Well, we don't want to be late. I promised the bowling league a look at Julia in a dress, so we have to make an extra stop at Lincoln Lanes."

"Paul!" my mother said, covering her mouth and blushing like a . . . well, like a middle-school girl.

I cleared my throat. "Your coat, Mother? And about that curfew . . ."

"Not to worry, Franklin." Penny walked over and put her arm around me. "We have it all taken care of. It just so happens that I am free tonight, and they're showing all the old Lassie movies at the Wealthy Theater. We won't get home until after eleven."

Paul opened the door for my mother and stood back.

"You're not going to start opening doors for me, are you?" she asked him. But you could tell she liked it.

Honestly, after three Lassie movies, I think I'm going to have to nominate Timmy to replace Stuart Little as the most accident-prone character in literature. I mean, how many ravines can one kid fall down?

Timmy wasn't the only one in mortal danger over the weekend. As I reviewed my school planner on Sunday afternoon, I recalled that it had been Sarah's weekend to have custody of our baby.

"Where's Keds?" I asked as soon as I saw Sarah outside science class on Monday.

Sarah hitched her thumb over her shoulder. "Takin' a nap."

"In your backpack?"

Sarah pulled me into the classroom, dropped her backpack unceremoniously on the floor, and began rummaging through it. I glimpsed Keds upside down, sandwiched between *Ven Conmigo* and *Science Interactions*.

"I got something for you." She pulled out a wrinkled plastic Megamart bag and pushed it at me.

"A present?"

"Nah. It's just something . . . well, in case I . . . I can't go with you . . ." Sarah bent over to zip her pack. "Go on, Franklin."

I thought about mentioning that our health grade might be compromised if Keds had ink stains on his face, but I was overcome by a sudden wave of feeling: Sarah Kervick had purchased something for me. And it was in a store bag, which meant she actually paid money for it.

"Well, look at it."

I peeked in the bag and pulled out a CD entitled *Water Sounds*.

"I know you have a player. You even have a special pocket at the top of your backpack." She reached over my shoulder to yank on the zipper, but I pulled away. The CD-player compartment was where I kept my stash of Mercurochrome and antibacterial hand wipes.

"You can go in the john, in the stall, and turn this on. They got waves, waterfalls, river rapids. It'll work, don't worry."

"But where will you be?"

Sarah took a long breath and let it escape through her nose. "Oh yeah. There's something else. It blew off her head the other day and I nabbed it."

I looked down at the wrinkly piece of fabric Sarah pulled out of her pocket.

"That's not . . ."

"Yup. Glynnis' head thing. You really should give it back to her, Franklin."

I wondered what Glynnis' kerchief would say if it could talk. Did it go home with Sarah Kervick and eat dinner in front of the television set? Visit the dogs? I took the crumpled square of cotton from Sarah and folded it as best I could before stuffing it in my backpack.

Sarah tossed hers over her shoulder and pushed past me. I followed her. The alcove created by the skeleton and the jars of vital organs gave us a little privacy as other students streamed past.

"Why wouldn't you be able to go with me? Is something wrong, Sarah?"

Sarah looked at me, sizing me up. She swept her hand across her forehead, pushing back the hair that had fallen over her eyes.

"He lost his job again . . . at the door-panel factory."

My first thought was to ask why. But did it matter? There were so many possibilities: drinking, fighting, smoking around volatile chemicals.

"That's not his only job," I said, finally.

"Oh, c'mon, Franklin. And he fell asleep, by the way. He couldn't help it."

*I'm sure he couldn't.*

Class was set to begin. Sarah gave me a searching look, as if I might have some ideas for how to restore her father's job. "Let me think," I told her. "We'll talk about it later, after class." My attention was drawn to the front of the room, where someone was humming the "Happy Birthday" song. I took my seat and observed Mr. Spansky standing at the sink, his back to us, energetically washing his hands.

But later never came. Even after school, as we sat together in the backseat on our way to pick up Sarah's costume, there was never a good time. Penny was up front. She was anxious to see Sarah's costume since my mother had convinced her to do Sarah's makeup for the exhibition.

As we drove, Penny chattered about the girls'—that is, her dogs'—latest exploits while Sarah stared glumly out the window. Though I was hoping to review the articles I'd printed off the Internet during free time in the media center, I found myself instead stealing glances at Sarah.

I had no experience with the situation she was in. My mother's job seemed quite secure. Cable access was not going away. When it did, she would get trained in the new technology. They needed small, flexible types in her kind of work. She had worked for Cable Country for seven years. Before that it was ComTrast.

Since Penny was in attendance, I was not required to enter the filthy home of Fiona Foster. As soon as my mother, Penny, and Sarah exited the van, I settled in to review the latest findings of the American Council of Cheerleading Coaches and Advisors, or ACCCA. I was shocked to discover that, according to at least one report, more than half the catastrophic injuries to females during the high school and college years involve cheerleading accidents.

Could Glynnis be in danger? The research suggested that the girls highest on the pyramid were the most likely to suffer injury. I thought of Glynnis and her slender frame, her rounded shoulders, her soft elbows. My mind took a very unscientific turn then as I imagined our clean hands clasped together on the school steps, as I had observed certain eighth graders doing that very morning before the bell.

I reached into my backpack for the crumpled kerchief. I sniffed it, wondering if I could distinguish the scent of Glynnis from all the other scents it must have picked up over the last few days. But all I could pick up was the faint smell of smoke. Sigh. Despite my fantasies, Glynnis and I seemed to get further apart by the day. Still, I would have to return this kerchief, and, at least, Glynnis would know what I was capable of in the laundering and ironing department when that happened.

"I'm wondering," I began as my mother got back in the driver's side, "if we could have a talk later tonight about, well . . ." I trailed off. "Just a chat."

But my mother did not hear me. "I have reservations about this," she said, tossing a cardboard box onto the backseat for Sarah. "You're sure it's okay with Debbi?"

"She said for the exhibition," Sarah responded, keeping her head down.

I tried again. "As I was saying . . ."

"Sorry, Franklin. What?"

"I think it opens up interesting possibilities," Penny interrupted us, climbing into the van. My mother started the engine and used one hand to execute a three-point turn.

"And what might those be?"

"Well, I know it's not the traditional—"

"I'm not arguing about it, I just said I have reservations." My mother stopped talking to concentrate on flying around an elderly woman, who—according to a quick mental rate-of-speed calculation—was driving the speed limit. "You know, in all these competitions and exhibitions, have you ever seen a girl in pants?"

"It is different, I'll give you that. But it does have possibilities. That's all I'm saying."

Sarah was not participating in the conversation. She stared straight ahead, concentrating on the back of my mother's seat.

The natural question was, *Why* is Sarah competing in

pants? But my mother and Penny seemed to be well beyond the "why" and into the "how." I sighed and put my research back into the folder I'd cryptically labeled: WGP, for "Winning Glynnis Powell."

"Can we just stop back at your house for a couple minutes?" Penny asked my mother. "I'll have her try it on for me. I might have an idea."

Glancing in the rearview mirror and seeing how miserable Sarah looked must have made my mother rethink her stand.

She rallied with: "It's not that big a deal, really. Maybe Sarah will start a new trend."

At this, Penny laughed heartily, but Sarah didn't even look up. As the car slowed up in our driveway, she had one foot out the door. I had no idea what to make of this new version of Sarah. I was startled to realize that a part of me longed for the old mess-with-me-and-I'll-rearrange-your-body-parts version.

After we'd entered the house, Penny sent Sarah and the box down the hall before turning to my mother.

"Julia, I'm going to need a measuring tape."

My mother went over to the kitchen counter and flipped open the lid of her toolbox. She tossed Penny a metal container.

Penny stood there, yanking on the tab. "It's for a body, not a piece of lumber, girl. Haven't you got a sewing kit? I need straight pins, too."

My mother replied by raising one eyebrow and giving Penny an ultimatum: "It's that or a yardstick. As for pins, I've got a couple of safety pins in the junk drawer." She grabbed two cereal boxes from the cupboard and smacked them onto the table. As I watched her pull milk from the refrigerator, spoons from the drawer, and bowls from the drainer by the sink, I got the sinking feeling this would be dinner. I was about to remind her that I preferred soy milk, but my mother plunked down in her chair as if this was the last move she would make for a while.

Penny was still waiting.

"I have a measuring tape on my bedpost and a travel sewing kit in my top desk drawer," I said, trying to move things along. I was about to request politely that she remove her shoes before entering my bedroom, but Penny anticipated my comment with: "Don't worry, I'll take off the shoes, Franklin."

Before she left the room, Penny stopped behind my mother's chair and tried to knead her shoulders.

"It's just my opinion, but I think you should lighten up, Julia."

My mother leaned to one side so that she could look Penny in the eye. "You do."

"She's just a kid."

"She should have told me sooner. It might have been serious."

"But she didn't. It was a mistake. You're her hero, Julia. Be a hero and forgive her."

My mother responded to this by pouring milk into her cereal bowl. She always put the milk in first. It was her invention for keeping the cereal dry. Finally, Penny left and there we were, across the kitchen table from each other and separated by a box of Bran Buds and her glowing neon container of Lucky Charms.

"Is anyone ever going to tell me what's going on around here?" I asked her. "Or do I have to keep tuning into the mystery that has become my life to find out episode by episode? Since when do they let girls compete in pants?"

Two spoonfuls of cereal went into my mother's mouth in quick succession.

"I am, after all, part of the team. I go to her practices, I help her with homework, I . . . I worry about her, too."

"Seriously?"

"Yes, Mother. Seriously."

My mother pushed the mass of half-chewed cereal to one side of her mouth so that she could make herself understood. "She was burned, Franklin. On her leg. And she didn't want anybody to know about it."

"Burned? As in . . ."

"As in she spilled the hot water from boiling hot dogs on her leg. At least, that's what she tells me."

I tried to piece it together. "So that's why she didn't want to wear a skirt? But wouldn't her tights have covered it?"

"You should see the scar. It must have hurt like the dickens. She said she couldn't stand having the tights next to it. And she was afraid someone might see her if she had to change in the locker room."

"But why would that be a big deal? It's not like Sarah Kervick's injuries haven't been on display before."

"But an injury like this one . . . well, people might ask questions, Franklin. They might wonder about her home life. Sarah puts a fair amount of energy into protecting . . ." My mother's spoon stopped midway to her mouth. She let it drop back to the table before pushing the bowl away. ". . . her father. If someone suspected Sarah was abused, they might separate them."

"Abused? But you don't think he—"

Big sigh. "Honestly, Franklin, I don't know what to think. Other than I'm pretty much out of my league here."

I sat down in my chair, considering. "Have you told Gloria?"

"She knows. We're working on it. But wait, you wanted to talk to me about something, didn't you? In the car, you said . . ."

It hardly seemed fitting to bring up Glynnis at a time like this.

"It's nothing."

"No, really. Go ahead." She leaned forward as if determined to put her all into this one. As if what I was about to say might be a problem she could actually solve.

I decided to give it a try. "All right. Mother, there comes a time in every boy's life when he is not so much a son as he is, well . . . look here, Mother. I have pledged my affections to another woman. Glynnis Powell, to be exact."

"Who is Glynnis Powell?"

"The girl who won the Principal's Penmanship Award last year. Don't you remember? I was runner-up."

"The skinny one? With the bandana on her head?"

My mother reached behind her for the bowl of fruit and began to peel an apple with the same utility knife she used on the job.

"I think it's called a 'kerchief.' "

"Okay? The skinny one with the kerchief on her head? Does she know?"

Spearing a slice of apple with the tip of her knife, she held it out, offering.

I shook my head no. "I think we should be friends at first," I told her. "I want to invite Glynnis to sit with us at lunch."

"Sounds like a good plan . . . but don't think too hard about it. . . ." Here, she pointed her knife in my direction and continued sternly: "If there's one thing I've learned about love, it's that you can't think too hard."

This, coming from my mother, would be the obvious conclusion.

# CHAPTER TEN

# Flour Power

I made little progress in my campaign to win Glynnis Powell over the next week. Even though I kept her kerchief, laundered and ironed with spray starch and lavender water, in the top zippered compartment of my backpack, events conspired to keep us apart. Well, that, and acute attacks of shyness that hit just as I was within greeting distance. But I had plenty of time to ponder my mother's oh-so-wise advice. On the day of Sarah's exhibition, for example, I found myself sitting *alone* at the end of my table in the low-traffic area of the cafetorium and, for the one hundredth time that day, thinking about not thinking about Glynnis.

I cast a longing glance in the direction of the cheerleaders' table. There sat Glynnis, her flour baby on her lap. I wondered what she did with the child during cheerleading practice. If she made sure her team practiced all towers and pyramids on the two-inch foam surface recommended by the ACCCA, there might be a corner left for a baby blanket. The intensity of my stare drew her attention. How could it not? She covered her mouth with her napkin and blushed. I hoped my return blush was as bright as hers.

Sighing, I inserted my sandwich back into its biodegradable cellulose bag. Truly, I felt alone in all the world. Bernie was in

Gary, Indiana, inspecting ranches and split-levels, though he was due back this afternoon. Sarah Kervick was doing whatever she did wherever she did it. She would catch up with me following the final bell on the sidewalk outside of school, a trick she often employed when we were supposed to walk home together.

My priority at the moment was to make it through a bathroom episode unscathed.

After packing up my things, I clutched my CD of water sounds to my chest and headed to the exit that led to the boys' bathroom by the gym.

"Hey, Donut-brain. Where's your girlfriend?" Marvin Howerton shouted just as I was in sight of safety. Half the cafetorium quieted to hear my response.

And how should I respond to this oh-so-clever permutation of my name? With honesty?

*Fair, fresh, and sensibly attired, she sits among us.*

No. We all knew who Marvin was referring to. I chose not to escalate tensions by remaining silent. As if he'd conjured her up, Sarah Kervick came bustling toward me as soon as I'd reached the hall. Keds was tucked under her arm like a football.

She grabbed me roughly by the elbow and propelled me to our destination.

The bathroom entrance was blocked by the orange cones that signal CAUTION: WET FLOOR. Sarah ignored them and pushed me through the door; I narrowly missed a concussion-inducing blow from Mr. Herman's broomstick.

Just as roughly, she pulled me back into the hall and whispered, "He's not done yet."

Indeed, Mr. Herman appeared to be in some kind of a trance, his back to us, moving like a cat across the bathroom floor. The broomstick had been unscrewed from the broom end, and now he jabbed it like a bayonet, swung it in an arc over his head, and brought it low with fierce strokes over the surface of the floor.

"He's practicing," Sarah whispered.

"Practicing for what?" I asked her. "Mortal combat?"

"Weapons class. He already has a third-degree black belt. He has to learn weapons for the next one."

With a flourish, Mr. Herman landed the broom handle into the broom and quickly screwed the two pieces together. He swept a few strokes for a cooldown before looking up and acknowledging our presence. His dark skin glistened with sweat.

"Hey," Sarah said, "okay if we . . ." She tossed her head at me, and I understood at once that she had told Mr. Herman everything.

Sarah set Keds—*our baby*—on the counter next to the sink. When Mr. Herman turned and saw what she'd done, he scooped up the bag and put it on the paper-towel dispenser.

"I just washed that counter," he said. "It's wet."

It was on the tip of my tongue to ask if he would perch his own baby on a paper-towel dispenser, but Sarah had moved in close so that she could whisper.

"Really," she said. "I asked him if it was okay . . . to help you."

Despite the pressure I was experiencing, I was able to observe how tired she looked: Her face was pale; she had dark circles under her eyes.

Sarah put her hand on my shoulder. "He comes here every day on his lunch hour to practice."

Mr. Herman took his time collecting his bucket and mops. Finally, he left us, rolling the cart in front of him. Every fiber of my being told me to toddle over to the bathroom stall and "make water," as the cowboys say, but the things that were happening to Sarah Kervick lately exerted another sort of pressure in the area of my chest. Was it fear? Sadness? I couldn't rightly tell.

"Isn't there anything we can do to help, Sarah? Whatever it is, my mother has a way . . ."

She turned around and began drawing little patterns on the wet counter with her finger. "It's just . . . it never mattered before . . . when we'd leave."

"But why would you have to? There are lots of factories. Your dad can get another job."

Sarah smiled her old smile, the kind where her lips stay pressed together. She adjusted my headphones and pushed me—not hard—into the stall.

"It's more than that," she told my back as I disappeared into the stall. "And I might . . . maybe . . . need your help. We'll see, but thanks, Franklin. You're all right. I used to think you were a bean head when I first met you, but I know different now. You're all right."

I stood on the other side of the metal door, fumbling with my zipper and trying to picture a Sarah Kervick problem I could possibly resolve.

"If I, you know . . . you should tell her if . . ."

Sarah was talking, but I must admit at the moment I was

caught up in the delirious relief of waves crashing to the shore. I emerged from the stall and pulled off the earphones, prepared to ask her to repeat herself. But I didn't get the chance.

"Look, it's Donut-hole. I said they'd be here, didn't I?"

"What kinda twisted . . ."

Bryce and Marvin had burst through the door and taken us completely by surprise.

"Hey, Bryce," Marvin said, laughing and scooping up Keds. "They're makin' Donut-babies." He tossed our sack of flour to Bryce, but it was snagged midair like a hard fly that had crested the second baseman's glove and landed in Sarah's territory. She shoved Keds into my breadbasket and squared off to take on Bryce and Marvin.

I'm afraid the combination of wet counter and excessive force proved too much for our doomed offspring. What was first a trickle became a gush and, within seconds, the inner cavity of our baby landed on my shoes, covering me in flour from navel to toes.

Rather than make an attempt to salvage our assignment, Sarah took advantage of the fact that Marvin and Bryce were pointing and laughing, and scooped up two handfuls of flour and proceeded to blind our enemies. This set in motion a chain of events that left four sixth-grade bodies completely covered in refined carbohydrates. Marvin Howerton reinjured his instep, Bryce Jordan's nose spurted blood, and Sarah's left cheek and eye cracked against The Bowl, resulting in an impressive shiner.

I, too, sustained an injury: a nasty bruise on my elbow where the bathroom-stall door banged into me in my hurried attempt to get back to safety.

Since we all bore the telltale signs of a skirmish, we were sent directly to Principal Kluhaski's office by Miss Zammit, our art teacher, who was standing conveniently outside the bathroom, her arms full of Chinese good-luck symbols created during lunchtime calligraphy practice.

The story we told could not be considered a passing acquaintance with the truth, and I found that I would have time to repent at leisure in the company of other juvenile-delinquents-in-training in after-school detention.

But I had little time to reflect on these traumatic events, because it was the *very day* of Sarah Kervick's first public performance, the skating "dress rehearsal" where young competitors were encouraged to perform their routines in full costume in front of a crowd of admiring friends and relatives.

More difficult by far was the preshow appearance with my mother in our kitchen. Under the glare of fluorescent lighting—which I have repeatedly tried to get my mother to change to the warmer, broad-spectrum hues that imitate sunlight—Sarah Kervick's injury looked pronounced. I think it is safe to say that she appeared to be returning from a tristate tour with the Women's Wrestling Federation.

My mother took one look at Sarah, sank into a kitchen chair, and laid her head on her folded arms. She then proceeded to have a muted conversation with the table surface that included the phrase "Why me?"

Without lifting her head, she reached for the cell phone latched to her belt and speed-dialed Penny.

"Are you on your way? Good. Maybe you'll get here before I commit a crime," she said.

In less than two minutes, Penny burst through the door, took a long look at Sarah's face, and whistled through her teeth. She handed Sarah her sewing bag and patted her purse.

"Lucky for me, I spent a year at the Chic Institute for Cosmetology before I discovered my gift for court reporting. We did a whole unit on reconstructive surgery. Go on to the rink," she said, shooing us away. "I'll get her ready, don't worry."

Sarah turned to go down the hall. She cast a longing backward look at my mother.

"Just think about your performance for now, okay?" my mother told her. "We'll talk about the flour incident . . . later."

My mother consulted her watch. "Oh man, I'm late. I was supposed to be there by now."

Why my mother had to be at the rink at all hours was a mystery worth pondering when my blood pressure returned to the normal range.

"Well, go then. We'll meet you," Penny said.

I sent a nonverbal distress signal to my mother. She was so entangled in other people's lives these days, I wasn't sure she'd still be capable of picking one up. I *did not* approve of Penny's driving. She applied lipstick at busy intersections, and was forever inserting her nail file into her tape player to jiggle loose one of her Grateful Dead recordings. This caused her to lose eye contact with the roadway for seconds at a time.

My mother looked at me, looked at her watch again, and sighed. "All right," she said. "But hurry up and change. I am not showing up there with the Pillsbury Doughboy."

Up in my room, I stripped my clothes, applied stain stick to a mysterious blob on the sleeve of my shirt before laying it carefully in my laundry basket, and quickly donned long underwear and a muffler in anticipation of the freezing temperatures at the ice rink.

As I cast a longing backward glance at my sanctuary, I realized—to my horror—I'd forgotten to remove my shoes. Floury footprints revealed my movements, and my neglected tape measure swayed slightly on my bedpost as a result of my recent activity.

"All right," my mother announced in the car. "We're going to come clean. No more secrets—" She fell silent, diverted by something in the rearview mirror. I craned around to see a boy riding his bike without a helmet. As we approached the corner, I realized it was Bernie, pedaling furiously to catch up with us. My mother stomped on the brake.

"Sorry, guy, I forgot we were giving you a ride," she said, leaping out of the van and grabbing Bernie's bike. "Let's toss it in the back."

Once we were under way again, I disregarded my vital signs and plunged in: "Does coming clean mean that you tell us exactly what occupies your time at the skating rink? Either you have secret meetings with Paul behind the Zamboni, or you're in training for a tour with the Women's Wrestling Federation."

"I thought we were going to start with you telling me what really happened this afternoon."

"I think we should unravel our mysteries in chronological order."

My mother eyed Bernie in the rearview mirror. "Are you sure you want to know?"

"Yes!"

"I have to clean the bathrooms."

"Excuse me?"

"That's how they afford the ice time," Bernie chimed in. "And the coaching."

My mother nodded. "Even with Gloria's help, it's awful expensive."

"Tell me, does the rest of the neighborhood know my mother is a janitress, or are our casual acquaintances as in the dark as I am?"

"I knew you'd make a big deal out of it," my mother said, making a rolling right turn at a red light and proceeding without regard for the speed of the oncoming vehicles. "It just came up. Paul knew that the woman who usually cleans at night was going to be off for a hip replacement, so I asked Win Davies, the rink manager, if he thought I could do the work in exchange for Sarah's ice time. . . ."

I began making a mental list of the germs my mother had been coming in contact with over the last several months. In public bathrooms, strains of bacteria can meet and mingle, forming new, mutant strains that confound our limited arsenal of antibiotic defense.

"Do you realize, Mother—"

"Spare me, Franklin."

Bernie patted my shoulder. "I wish my mother was like yours, Franklin. It's not like my mother helps anybody achieve their dreams. All my mother does is sell Amway products."

"Merilee gave us a great deal on bathroom cleanser, and

Win knocked the difference off Sarah's coaching bill. It was Bernie's idea."

"But why didn't you tell me?"

"Because I didn't want to worry you, Franklin. Honestly, if I told you the details of my work life, you'd probably never sleep again. And it's *not* because my jobs are dangerous."

Once again, I found myself in the perplexing situation of making my mother upset for pointing out that the lifestyle she had chosen was not optimally designed to avoid risk. What was so wrong with trying to avoid bad things?

And yet, in the case of the bathroom cleaning, the hygiene hypothesis could also be argued. Here my mother was warring with germs on a daily basis and winning. *She* did not suffer from allergies, asthma, or lactose intolerance.

As we pulled up to the arena entrance, my mother handed me her cell phone. Bernie extracted his camcorder from his backpack. We got out of the van and watched her speed to the back of the lot to park near Paul's truck before we turned to enter the rink under the menacing sign, SKATE AT YOUR OWN RISK. I made a mental substitution, replacing *skate* with *live*. It was beginning to feel like my anthem.

As we took our seats, Bernie talked a blue streak, something about his queen and her recent perils. I checked for Gloria's number on speed dial, and watched my mother's boyfriend demonstrate his special talent for driving in circles. Sitting atop his Zamboni, Paul had only a T-shirt and a plaid shirt to protect him from the cold. I slapped my thighs, thinking of the relative warmth of the snack area, yet remembering my mother's order to save her a good seat. We would be here for a while.

"But she has lots of ideas. She thinks it's one of those lists you could even syndicate," Bernie was saying as he panned the audience with his camera. "Like that little column in the newspaper, 'News of the Weird.' People like to read that stuff."

I looked over at Bernie and tried to appear interested. "Uh-huh."

"Glynnis says we should add nursery-rhyme characters too, like Jack, who's always jumping over the candlestick. Or that Wee Willie Winkie, who runs all over town . . . he's just asking for it, Glynnis says."

At the mere mention of her name, I felt the color rise to my face.

"You and Glynnis have talked about our list of characters in literature? The ones most likely to die in preventable accidents?" I asked Bernie, to confirm that we were indeed talking about the same thing.

"Yup." He nodded. "Glynnis thinks we should do more medieval stuff. You know, like *Robin Hood* and *The Sword in the Stone*. She's big into knights and princesses."

With its lack of sanitation, modern medicine, and adequate nutrition, medieval literature had presented a challenge so great it threatened to overwhelm our database. However, with a new research partner, it might not be such an impossible task.

The stands began to fill with heavily padded friends and relatives. I saw Mr. and Mrs. Perkins arrive with Miss Mathews, who was in a tight-fitting parka and warm-up pants.

"Look, it's Mrs. Boardman!" Bernie said, waving his free

arm wildly. "And Mr. Putnam, too." It was indeed our old principal, helping our old library aide to a seat in the bleachers. Mrs. Perkins was right. Sarah Kervick would have a cheerleading section.

Though it was close to time to begin, the skaters were nowhere to be seen. I knew from past exhibitions that they were closeted in the changing rooms, hot curling irons dangerously close to their temples, eyelash curlers at the ready. It was lucky for Sarah that skaters wore heavy stage makeup for these events so that their features could be seen from a distance. Penny would have to do a pretty good plaster job to cover up that bruise.

I shuddered to think of Penny working over Sarah Kervick's face. There was a twinge of sympathetic pain for her injury, but also concern over Penny's general lack of hygiene. She might have run her dogs and grabbed a variety of public door handles since she last washed her hands. Now she'd be licking her fingers and erasing any mistakes on Sarah's face with her own saliva. It is a simple fact that more than two hundred thousand cases of eye injury seen in ERs across the country are due to misuse and misapplication of makeup.

My mother took the bleachers two at a time, breathless and red faced.

"Have you seen Sarah's dad?" she asked, wedging herself between me and Bernie.

"Nope." Bernie trained his lens on my mother, who immediately pushed it away.

"Save the film for Sarah."

As if on cue, four costumed girls burst onto the ice and began stroking to warm up. Sarah was not among them, and yet we'd been told she was in the first flight, or group, to perform.

"Penny says Sarah's not going to warm up on the ice," my mother said when I tugged on her sleeve. "They want to rely on the element of surprise."

"No warm-up?" I repeated. "Need I remind you of the increased risk of injury—"

"She's young, Franklin." As if this settled everything, my mother shrugged off her jacket and waved to Paul, who was wiping the shaved ice off the front of his vehicle.

"What order did she draw?"

"Fifth."

There is a definite psychology to the order you draw in skating competitions. It's not good to go first. Even the crowd is not warmed up. It doesn't do to go last. That gives you too much time to get nervous. It's best to be settled in the very middle of the second or third flight. Sarah was skating last in the first flight, the positive and negative implications of which I could spin out endlessly.

But since this was an exhibition, the girls would not yet be judged, and I did not need to trouble myself about such things. Not all the normal rules of competition applied. Skaters were allowed props, for example. Most of the skaters were simply doing a dress rehearsal of the program they'd skate for the regional competition in a little over a week. But a few took the opportunity to explore their more creative side. The first skater to go, for instance, had a cowboy theme. She wore her hair in stiff braids under a hat that frequently blew off during high stroking. The possibilities for impaired vision and uneven drag clearly outweighed whatever charm points she might be making by donning the hat. That was my humble opinion, anyway.

Other than that, I have very little recollection of the first four skaters. In addition to the cowgirl, there was one with musical notes on her skirt who performed a mediocre routine to "Stardust." Penny joined us in the bleachers as an "All That Jazz"–themed skater finished her program.

"Better call Gloria now," my mother advised.

It had been my idea to arrange a phone call to Gloria during Sarah's performance. No matter how well Sarah did, Gloria deserved to share in this moment.

"Gloria Nelots here."

"Gloria? It's me, Franklin."

"You don't have to shout, Franklin."

We were forced to pause as the crowd erupted in cheers at the conclusion of some sort of Tinkerbell program skated by a rather robust fairy in a tiara and a tulle skirt.

"It's almost time," I told her after the noise had died down.

"For Sarah to skate?"

I listened for the telltale signs of Gloria relaxing. Of coffee being poured over crackling ice cubes, of the dull thud of her surely sensible shoes settling on her desk, but all those details were lost in the surrounding noise.

"I need a little help here, Franklin. I'm sitting next to a stack of reports on the dangers of young people ages six to twelve being left unattended after school. Bring me into your world, would you?"

There was a time when I would have recited the statistics on skating injuries, the tears in the rubber mat, the sharp edges of the metal seats, but I knew Gloria did not want that. Just as in other areas of my life, my job description seemed to be changing. I was to put a positive spin on the day. I thought back over the disaster with the costume, Sarah's bruised cheek, my mother's new occupation as a custodian. I thought hard.

"Frankin? Are you speechless? Set the stage!" Gloria barked, loud enough for the spectators around us to hear.

"Give me that," my mother said, and unceremoniously yanked the phone out of my hand.

"Hey, Gloria, it's me, Julia. Let's see. Sarah's up, but we don't have a clear view from here of where she enters the rink. I'd say there are about a hundred people in the stands. I can see Debbi across the rink, holding up a cassette tape to make sure she's got the right one. . . ."

Penny reached over and poked me while my mother talked. "We had to make a few costume changes to cover the injury," she whispered. "Keep your fingers crossed!"

I thought of the girl in the cowboy hat. "What sort of changes?"

"Just wait."

My mother was so busy describing our environs that she completely missed Paul at the bottom of the bleachers and his thumbs-up sign. Bernie and I stood to get a better view as Sarah stepped onto the rink. As she skated toward the center, my mother broke off in midsentence, yet another member of the Donuthead clan to be rendered speechless.

# CHAPTER ELEVEN

# Olé

Instead of wearing just simple pants and a full shirt—the typical boy costume she had chosen from Fiona Foster's metal ready-made cabinet—Sarah Kervick, now looking both exotic and intimidating, had on the tight-fitting jacket of a Spanish bullfighter, a jet-black cape lined in red satin, and a Zorro-like mask to cover her bruised face. Penny had pulled Sarah's long blond hair into a high, tight ponytail that glistened as it fell down the back of the cape. My mind immediately went to the possible drag on her momentum this might cause. This cape would be far heavier than a dime-store cowboy hat.

"Get a load of Sarah," Bernie said, sighing. "I gotta make a new character for that."

The hand holding the phone dropped to my mother's lap as her eyes followed Sarah Kervick gliding to the center of the rink.

I took it gently from her and said, "Gloria . . . um . . ." into the receiver as Sarah executed a couple of strong crossovers, extended her right leg behind her, and came to a T-stop in the center of the rink.

"Franklin? What's going on over there? Franklin? Did Sarah fall?"

"Sarah's wearing a cape, Gloria. And a mask. She looks like a . . . cross between El Zorro and a bullfighter."

"We just picked it up at Costume Castle," Penny explained to my mother.

"...it is an exhibition," Gloria was saying. "I thought you said the girls were allowed some creativity."

"I said she's wearing a cape, Gloria. She's never practiced with a cape so far as I know." *Not unless she and Penny had been going over it in the parking lot, for Pete's sake!*

Like my mother, I lost all capacity for speech. The crowd had fallen into a hushed and expectant silence. Debbi was so shocked by Sarah's appearance that she stood there, tape in hand, as if she'd forgotten her role as maestro. Sarah was frozen in place, waiting for the music.

Someone needed to break this tension.

I stood and shouted a rousing "Olé!"

Several mittened mothers turned around to stare at me. Bernie was all over it.

"Olé!" he shouted over and over, ruining whatever potential there was for a quality sound track on his video. Debbi managed to jab the tape into the cassette player.

As the music crackled to life, Gloria said, "You might want to warn me next time you decide to *shout into the phone...*"

"Sorry, Gloria," I said. "I'm all business now. Okay, she's stroking... and she's gliding... can you hear the music? Okay, she's going into her first move. It's a single toe loop. Wait a minute...."

I couldn't talk and process at the same time. My mother was cutting off the circulation in my thigh, squeezing in nervous anticipation. Instead of folding her arms into her body as she'd practiced a thousand times, Sarah Kervick let the cape fill with air. The lining created a brilliant red border to her body as she executed the toe loop, her body firm, her landing solid, her extension elegant.

"Have you seen her practice with that thing?" my mother asked me.

I shook my head.

Gloria's distant voice reached me as if from a dream.

"I'm warning you, Franklin. You have one more second . . ."

Bernie put down his camera and took the phone. "Hey, Gloria. It's me, Bernie," he said, as if they were close personal friends. "Okay, now I'm going to tell you. Sarah's racing around the rink. She's picking up speed. Looks like she's gonna jump . . ."

Of course, I knew Sarah's routine by heart. I knew that her next jump was a Salchow, and that led into a corkscrew spin. What I didn't know was how the added weight and drag of this heavy cape would affect my abilities to predict her moves—let alone hers to make them!

And yet, she skated on, completely unfazed, using the cape as a prop as if she'd been skating that way all her life. Now, in her corkscrew spin, Sarah folded it around her as neatly as an umbrella and then—with a flick—she flipped it into the air and released it.

And I do mean released. Buoyed by a cushion of air, it remained aloft for an amazing three revolutions. By the time it floated to the surface of the ice—satin side up—Sarah Kervick had made a clean getaway. The crowd burst into spontaneous applause.

As the music went into a crescendo, Sarah performed some

of the required dance moves, picking with the toe of her skate; performing a chassé; pivoting in a tight circle, one arm curved above her head, one finger snapping at her rib cage like a flamenco dancer's. Though the mask hid the expression on her face, her body moved in the same liquid, languid way it did when she was fully content and performing her death-defying activities without the slightest hint of fear.

Sarah's next several moves took her to the edges of the rink. But soon she would have to return to the center, and I began calculating the adjustments necessary to avoid the circle of red satin that now sat like a bull's-eye in the middle of the ice.

You could feel the tension build as Sarah skated backward toward the obstacle. You *have* to skate backward to enter a lutz jump. In the same way that she routinely turned her back on Marvin Howerton when he was still in striking range, Sarah Kervick skated backward on a collision course with her own cape. At the very last moment possible, she extended both arms and her back leg and broke free of gravity's hold at the edge of that circle of satin, performing her single lutz right over it. There was a communal intake of breath. In the silence, Gloria could be heard speaking sternly to Bernie: "I said put Franklin back on," then thunderous applause as Sarah Kervick landed her jump and transitioned all that energy into a camel spin, a pull-up blade spin, and then a sudden cessation of movement with a front T-stop.

*Olé.*

The crowd was on its feet. *Who is she?* seemed to ripple through the bodies straining to get a better look. I glanced down to see Mrs. Boardman waving her jiggly arms in the air. She was whistling through her teeth! My mother alternately grabbed me around the shoulder and punched Penny in the arm. Bernie gave her a high five. Paul was tossing roses onto the rink, and Sarah circled, picking them up and waving to the crowd.

My mother took the bleachers two at a time, rushing to the opening of the rink, where Sarah threw herself into my mother's arms, panting and laughing. My mother tugged her ponytail and kissed the top of Sarah's head. Watching them, I had that stabbing feeling of sadness, the kind you get when you realize these people who make up your inner circle are closer to each other than they are to you.

It was the kind of feeling that would send me to the phone to speed-dial 1-800-555-SAFE.

Uh-oh.

"Bernie, where's the cell?"

"Huh?" Only Bernie Lepner could remove himself from the chaos of his surroundings to begin envisioning a flamenco-dancing bandito in his epic fantasy series. I heard a squeaky noise from below Bernie's thigh.

"Franklin? I hope you treat invited guests better than this. This was your idea, remember?"

Gloria had a few more choice things to say, but I felt it necessary to interrupt her.

"Gloria," I said slowly, "you would have been so proud. Sarah was . . . she was . . . perfect."

"Really?"

"Yes, really." The next skater had taken the ice, and her music made it hard, once again, to hear. "I'm sorry I didn't do a better job."

"Was her father there to see it?"

I glanced down at Sarah and my mother. It seemed like the same question had just occurred to them. They were scanning the bleachers, my mother's protective arm around her shoulder.

"I don't think so."

"I thought as much. All right, then, you are going to leave those abysmal bleachers and take me through it again, stroke by stroke. You owe me that much, Franklin."

# Defensive Pessimism

Sarah felt a pressing need to get home after her performance, so we agreed to wait until the following Tuesday to celebrate her amazing debut on the ice. As for the costume and the fighting, all was forgiven on every side. My mother thanked Sarah for protecting me, congratulated Penny on her masterful use of disguise, and even apologized for not being more understanding about Sarah's need to wear pants. As she looked at me in her spirit of expansive generosity, all she could think to say was, "You're a trouper, Franklin."

Trouper indeed. Unlike some people, I returned to school and soldiered on bravely, navigating the potential disasters with an attitude of defensive pessimism that I believe will help me attain a higher spot on the age index than most adolescents. You see, psychologists at Wellesley College have found that anxious types like me, whose low expectations of life have them planning for disaster at every turn, fare better than the cheerful among us (Bernie Lepner comes to mind here). Why? Because we prepare for the worst while *they*, with their don't-worry-be-happy way of life, fall headlong into disaster. I proved this theory correct the following day, when I changed my route and ducked into the bathroom near the computer lab.

There, assisted by the refreshing sound of the ocean surf through my earphones, I managed to complete my business without incident.

And so the days that followed Sarah Kervick's masterful display passed as peacefully as could be expected in a place like Pelican View Middle School. Sarah Kervick was not in school on Friday or Monday. Taken by itself, this was not unusual: Mondays and Fridays found her in attendance even less than midweek. But so much had happened to her lately that I wished she had a phone, so that I could call her just to make sure she was okay.

Thankfully, Bernie was back in the lunchroom, saving me from the humiliation of eating alone. Mr. Lepner had been less than pleased with the benefits package offered by the engineering firm that interviewed him, so I'd have Bernie with me for several more weeks at least. Glynnis was in her regular clothes: a crisp, white, button-down, oxford-cloth shirt and a sensible denim skirt whose flounce at the hem brought it a healthy one inch below the tips of her fingers—well within the guidelines laid out in the Pelican View Middle School dress code.

I felt a little flutter in my stomach every time her gaze turned in my direction, successfully ignoring the defensive pessimist in me who suggested that putting all my eggs in one basket was not a good plan.

For this was our most recent topic in health class: healthy vs. unhealthy love. Or, as Miss Mathews would say, "mature vs. immature love."

"We'll start by filling out this worksheet. My boyfriend and I did it last night, and it was *very* interesting. You need to think of at least two relationships to take through the checklist. You can do friends, brothers, sisters, parents, girlfriends . . ."

"Only two?" piped up Tommy Williams. "I don't know how I'm gonna pick."

"Yes, Tommy. Only two."

On this particular day, our teacher wore a pair of black velour bell-bottoms that skimmed her high-heeled boots. On top, she wore a wraparound sweater that was, well, formfitting.

I kept my head down and scanned Student Handout Six. I wished I could take Glynnis through twice. On one side of the page was a heart filled with the characteristics of mature love. On the other side, a fractured heart displayed the characteristics of immature love. As I scanned the list accompanying the fractured heart, I began to feel a tiny bit unwell.

1. You lose interest in former hobbies and activities.

*When was the last time I measured my arms and legs?*

2. You depend on this person for all good feelings.

*Surely not. I could eke out a good feeling from Gloria on occasion.*

3. You ignore the weaknesses of the other person.

*That was easy. Glynnis didn't have any.*

4. You are jealous of each other's friends and time.

*Did that red-and-white girl gang qualify as friends?*

5. You feel pressure to go against your personal beliefs.

*Hadn't I entertained notions of inviting Glynnis with me to Perkins' Drug Store for a milk shake?*

I sat back and sighed. This new information was troubling. As I flipped over the page, I felt a surge of hope that we would find many more similarities here in the mature-love category. But how could I encourage Glynnis in her hobbies and ambitions when I didn't know what they were? Was our interest in caring for each other mutual and responsible? I could only vouch for my side of the equation on that one. Would Glynnis respect my values? We'd have to have a conversation first. Was I supportive of her activities and friendships? Well, only if they occurred above the two-inch dense foam recommended by the ACCCA. And even then, with reservations.

As I used my portable paper punch to ready the handout for my notebook, it struck me that every one of the qualities of mature love was exhibited by my mother toward Sarah Kervick. Did she not support Sarah in her goals, and respect her wishes? Was she not proud to introduce Sarah to her friends? They might need a bit of work on disagreeing constructively, but there was no doubt that their relationship landed them squarely within the intact heart of mutual admiration, respect, and affection.

Fabulous. Instead of me being ready to date Glynnis Powell, my mother and Sarah Kervick were the ones set to engage in a mature relationship.

"All right, then," Miss Mathews said, clearing her throat. "I need to collect your babies and the records you kept of the time you spent with them."

I cast a glance over my shoulder at Glynnis Powell and saw the same pained expression that I myself wore. Their baby sat crookedly on the desk in front of her, the marker eyes and mouth smeared, the brown bag spattered with dark stains.

I had reconstructed Keds using a bag of flour from my mother's pantry and a heavy application of transparent packing tape to the brown paper.

It was probably due to Miss Mathews' inexperience as a teacher that she allowed the whole class to comment on the condition of the babies without regard for the feelings of the other students. As she checked in with each pair, she held the baby up like an obstetrical nurse showing it off to a teary band of relatives.

"This bag is not creased at all. Look at how plump he is." She smiled at all of us . . . *relating*. "And this one here seems like she got excellent care. Oh look, you even read to her. Well, she's going to be a smart one.

"Tommy, what happened to your baby?"

Tommy Williams stood up, obviously relishing the opportunity for an audience.

"Well, it's like this, Miss Mathews. Tommy Jr. and I were having a little quality time in the lunchroom. . . . I was so busy taking care of his needs and all, I didn't notice that some joker had shook up my Coke . . ."

"You sprayed your infant son, your *namesake*, with Coca-Cola?"

"That gets the rust off pennies," Marvin Howerton added without raising his hand.

"Well, I . . ."

All eyes were on the jokester. Only I understood the pain this was causing Glynnis. Her normally excellent posture was slumped and defeated, her eyes downcast.

I felt the uncontrollable urge to act. My hand shot up. "Miss Mathews," I interjected. "It seems evident that in some cases the quality of the infant's care will vary wildly, depending on which parent he is with."

I was gratified by a look of obvious relief from Glynnis.

"Really, Franklin?" Miss Mathews came over to my desk.

"And who gets the credit for"—she scanned our sheet to find the baby's name—"Keds?"

The class burst into laughter, and I felt a piercing pang of embarrassment on behalf of our little one. I knew well how a name could color your world. Miss Mathews picked up Keds and ran her fingers along the creased expanse of packing tape that held the boy together.

"Well, Franklin?"

On a different day, in a different lifetime, I might have informed Miss Mathews that if I ever did have a baby with Sarah Kervick, I would not let the child out of my sight. But I had no intention of embarrassing Sarah. It was better to focus on the fact that I had removed the attention from Glynnis and, in an extremely mature act of love, contributed to her comfort by denying my own.

"The baby has had some early setbacks," I admitted. "It's nothing a little physical therapy can't cure."

"Really?" Miss Mathews turned the baby over, revealing his flour-bag bottom. "I've been wondering . . . Robin Hood brand? Hold Keds for a minute, won't you, Franklin?"

I got a sinking feeling as she walked back up the aisle to her desk. I don't know whether my blushing started as a result of Miss Mathews bending over to pluck something from her bottom desk drawer, or if it was in anticipation of future humiliations.

"As you know, all the babies in this assignment were born into Gold Medal flour bags. I just wonder if what you're handing in is not the baby you took home with you, and if this"—

Miss Mathews held aloft a splintered and splayed Gold Medal flour bag whose ragged ends were stiff with flour paste—"is the real Keds."

I hardly thought the heightened sense of drama with which she produced the evidence was necessary. Once again, I felt myself longing for a teacher who was not so eager to win the other students' approval. It was some comfort to see Glynnis through the laughing crowd, engaging in a sympathetic blush.

As we filed out of class, I felt the delicate touch of her hand on my shoulder.

"Oh, Franklin, I'm so sorry about . . . well, anyway, thank you for—" She broke off, unable to speak.

I smiled and bowed my head slightly. "It was nothing."

That was not the only upsetting incident of the day. The second one occurred in Mr. Spansky's science class. He was demonstrating the various properties of liquids and gases, and he held out a lit candle in one hand and a teaspoon full of crushed ice in the other. I noticed that he rocked back and forth slightly. One glance at his feet revealed two well-polished shoes beneath the knife-edge creases of his khaki pants. One shoe, however, had the sort of wedge you might see on a woman's sandal.

As I looked again at his face, I noticed that a little furrow of focus had appeared between his eyebrows. Did I not have that very same crease? I tentatively fingered the space just above the bridge of my nose, keeping my eyes on Mr. Spansky, who continued to have difficulty centering the spoon over the flame.

"It might be easier to center this if my legs weren't different lengths."

The combination of my mouth dropping open and Mr. Spansky's tongue being forced to enunciate a *th* and an *s* in quick succession produced a most unfavorable result.

Needless to say, I spent the next period in the nurse's office gargling with hydrogen peroxide and searching WebMD.com for the effects of foreign saliva being introduced into one's mouth. Though I was dismissed by Mr. Fiegel, I felt sick until the end of the day.

I honestly don't know whether my nausea was due to the fact that Mr. Spansky's spit bubble had come in contact with my tongue or my discovery that we had more in common than a tendency to be clean. One of his legs was shorter than the other!

In addition, we shared the same general build, and the same color of hair and eyes. Was it possible that the need to ensure lengthy contact between soap and water by singing the "Happy Birthday" song could be genetically encoded?

These disturbing thoughts followed me home. What I wanted to do was talk to Gloria, but her assistant, Miss Tweedell, said she was in a meeting until after four. That was too late.

At four o'clock, we were on our way to pick up Sarah for our celebration. Though I'd be relieved to know she was okay, I was not exactly in the mood to celebrate. Hadn't she abandoned me to navigate the hostile halls of Pelican View Middle these last days all on my own? What kind of partner is that? As we sat in the van, bouncing along in silence, I wondered if a restaurant named Bad Guys Pizza could have a clean health-inspection record. I also fretted, for the very first time, about whether discovering my father—my real, true, flesh-and-blood father—would be a disappointment; would, in fact, be worse than not knowing. Again, this was cause for a long and engaged discussion with Gloria. But, alas, it was time for an Al Capone pizza and a mobster milk shake.

As my mother pulled the van into the clearing, we both knew immediately that something was wrong. Very wrong. There was an eerie silence, for one thing. No barking dogs. No radio. No television. As we looked at each other and then at the yard in front of us, a gust of wind surrounded the van, stirring up a cloud of dust that swirled through the air toward Sarah's trailer and caught the screen door, banging it open.

I had never actually set foot inside Sarah Kervick's trailer. Now, as my mother pounded on the door and it swung inward at the pressure of her fist, I saw how small a space it really was. And how cold. It felt colder than being outside. One step and we were in the living room. A couch, a chair, both leaking foam, filled the space. A few more careful steps in one direction and we stood at the doorway to the bedroom. There was only one. In the other direction lay the kitchen. We looked around without speaking. It seemed like some great hand had taken hold of the Kervicks' possessions and dashed them up against the wall of the trailer. I had to tiptoe through a minefield: a rusted wrench, a *Car and Driver* magazine covered with oily fingerprints, a dirty athletic sock, an upended box of tooth-picks . . . it was very hazardous.

My mother made a noise that couldn't be categorized as belonging to the English language and headed for the kitchen.

"Wait a minute," I said. "Don't touch anything."

She squinted at me. "Why not?"

Any kid who has seen his share of cop shows would surely identify this as a crime scene. I gestured at the mess. "This seems like a matter for the police."

"Oh, please, Franklin," she said, pressing the heel of her hand against her eye. Was that a tear that glistened on her cheek? "For once, spare me the dramatics." She kicked at the kitchen chair that lay in her path. "Don't you remember what he said about never staying in one place long?"

"But the mess, surely . . ."

"It's called a quick getaway." After a glance into the tiny kitchen, she pushed past me and—to my horror—sat down on the chair. Something under the cushion made her reach beneath it. For her trouble, she was rewarded with one of Sarah Kervick's practice softballs, which she jammed into her jacket pocket.

She put her head in her hands, kneading her temples. "Knowing him, somebody else owns all this anyway."

The wind that rattled around the trailer carried with it a low keening noise, as if the great outdoors were expressing my mother's misery. She looked up at me in shocked surprise.

"Oh my God, Franklin, the dogs!" Rushing for the door, she kicked at a tangle of coat hangers and was gone before I could think of a reasonable argument to stop her.

Have I made it clear that Sarah's dogs did not hold the same place in my affections as in my mother's? Therefore, I did not rush headlong after her. Instead—to my surprise—I waded boldly into the bedroom. It was about the size of our laundry room, and clearly it belonged to Sarah. A narrow bed folded down from the wall and bumped up against an unfinished dresser. On the slice of wall between the tiny window and the bed, Sarah had taped pictures of women skaters she'd torn from the ridiculously overpriced "mag-alogs" my mother purchased for her at the skating rink. There was a photo, too. I had to sit on the bed to see it properly. Taken during my mother's camera-crazy phase last baseball season, it was a picture of me in my baseball uniform and my mother, a bat perched jauntily on her shoulder. There was something strange about the photograph . . . the ink had smudged across my mother's chest.

With my keen awareness of the physics of movement, I knew immediately—calculating the position of her body at rest, the arc of her arm, and the length of her fingers—that this was the spot where Sarah Kervick touched the picture before she went to sleep each night.

I sat there on that bed, not thinking about germs or potential injury from the rusting bed frame, not thinking at all, but *knowing* that a crime had been committed here. Because Sarah Kervick would not willingly leave without saying good-bye to my mother.

And then I saw something—a shape tangled in the blanket—that confirmed my suspicions. I tugged it up on my lap and unraveled the mess to reveal one of Sarah Kervick's figure skates.

I heard my mother's whistle, the one that had long ago called us in from the outfield at the Paul I. Phillips Recreation Center, and jumped up, reflexively hiding the skate behind my back. I was being summoned. I did not want my mother to see the skate. It was selfish, I know, but I had never seen my mother bawl before, and I wanted to be spared the trauma. For just as Franklin Delano Donuthead has principles to live by, we both knew that Sarah Kervick and her ice skates would never willingly be parted.

I couldn't leave it behind. I don't know why, but I just couldn't. I glanced wildly around the room, my gaze landing on Sarah Kervick's backpack in the corner, partially hidden under a worn . . . teddy bear? With a stealth I didn't know I was capable of, I stuffed the skate and, for some reason, the teddy bear into the backpack, which was already partially filled with assignments and books, and zipped it up. I hefted it onto my back—equally distributing the weight across both shoulders—and stepped carefully to avoid contact with anything that might have been handled by Kervick the Elder.

Outside, my mother stood in the dusty yard. She seemed to be studying the latest rusted heap Mr. Kervick was fixing up. It sat like some giant beast, its mouth propped open, the ever-present transistor radio swaying under the hood like a broken tooth.

"She said this would happen," my mother said quietly. "She said she would look up one day and I wouldn't be there." Pulling the softball out of her pocket, my mother tossed it in the air a few times as if feeling its weight. "I was really mad about it at the time, but Sarah was right. Tomorrow, she'll wake up and I won't be there."

With one swift move, she rocketed the softball at Mr. Kervick's radio, squarely meeting her mark and, through a handy demonstration of the transfer of energy, sent it flying into the dust.

I decided to take a proactive stance regarding the presence of Sarah Kervick's backpack.

"It's possible that Sarah will be in contact with me regarding her missed assignments," I said. Though this was about as likely statistically as being struck by lightning, she had to admit it *was* a possibility.

But my mother did not seem interested in the booty I had hauled from the Kervicks' trailer. She opened the van door and leapt in, adjusting her rearview mirror. I got in the passenger side, but as soon as I had buckled up, I froze in my seat.

"Mother, what is that smell?"

She placed her hands at ten and two o'clock on the steering wheel. *"That,"* she said, turning the key in the ignition, "is the probable result of half a dozen Thompson Treats on an empty stomach."

"Excuse me?"

"I couldn't leave them there, Franklin. I don't think they've eaten for a couple of days. We better go see Penny."

I hazarded a look into the back of the van at Pretzel and Zero, who lay in an exhausted heap on the floor. I could practically see the dander flying through the air, the fleas hopping. I pinched my nose.

"Surely there are places to call in a situation like this. . . ."

"Do you want to tell Sarah we took her dogs to the pound, Franklin? Would you like to be the one to make that call?"

Since Sarah Kervick was never available by phone, I knew this was a rhetorical question. My mother was not through.

"Have you ever been to the dog pound?"

"Have you?" I asked, calling her bluff.

"Well, not for years. But you only need to go once."

I was about as willing to turn my back on Sarah's mongrels as I was on Marvin Howerton. I jumped in my seat as one came to life, scratching its neck like mad. The other lay in a position of miserable abandon, its paws over its muzzle. As usual, I had no idea which one was which.

"Well, I suppose delivering them to Penny is the humane thing to do," I said, clutching Sarah's backpack to my chest.

On second thought, I put it on the floor at my feet.

# Call of Nature

The next day, I sat across the lunch table from Bernie and delivered the news about Sarah. For once, I had his attention.

"She's been abducted," Bernie said, dipping a breadstick into a concoction that advertisers market as "cheez" spread. With the sort of grades Bernie gets in spelling, he was the target audience for this clever presentation.

"By Dorgon Trolls, I suppose. This is serious, Bernie."

"No, really. Think about it. Sarah lives for skating," he said. "She would never leave town without her skates, Franklin...."

He broke off and stared into the middle distance, a look of wonder on his face.

"Franklin!" Bernie whacked his breadstick on the lunch table, his blob of "cheez" landing just short of my recently disinfected lunch area.

"This is like that story we read last year, *Honus and Me*. You have to return the skate to its rightful owner, just like he did that baseball card. You'll be a hero!" His voice had escalated to the point of attracting attention, not only from neighboring tables but from Mr. Fiegel himself.

"Lepner, Donuthead!" he barked into his bullhorn. "Volume!"

As fate would have it, my eyes were resting on the fair Glynnis Powell when Mr. Fiegel called out my name.

She looked up suddenly, her eyes finding mine across a sea of unsavory lunch trays. It was a balm sweeter than the organic pears canned in their own juice that sat, untouched, at my elbow.

"I can't believe you took in Zero, too. You know, Franklin, that's really out of character for you." Bernie gazed up at me through his filter of bangs with a look that bordered on admiration.

It made me feel somewhat relieved that he hadn't witnessed the scene I'd made when my mother attempted to bring the mongrel into the house. Penny had agreed to take in Pretzel, the female—who would have guessed?—but put her foot down at the idea of a male dog entering her home. Her other dogs had "masculine issues," she told us, as if that settled it.

"Mother, I cannot, in good conscience, allow you to invite this portable disease unit into the house that I have spent the better years of my life decontaminating."

"Franklin." She stood at the counter drinking coffee, an incredulous look on her face. "Haven't you read the research?"

"Research?"

"About SeDS?"

"SeDS?"

"Canines play a critical role in decreasing the odds of dying from Sedentary Death Syndrome."

A pitiful whining noise could be heard from the other side of the door. The hound was no longer in the garage but was sitting inside, his exposed rear end on the very same floor tiles I placed my laundry basket. I was torn between that unsavory image and what my mother had just said.

"Sedentary Death Syndrome?"

"Don't tell me you haven't heard of it."

"Well, it does sound familiar. . . ."

"Complications relating to inactivity, and deriving from obesity and heart disease, are the leading cause of death in this nation. They've eclipsed smoking, for heaven's sake. Don't play dumb with me, Franklin . . . the surgeon general is up in arms! People have to start moving. A daily walk with pets is a great way to begin a regular course of exercise. Now that you're not in a sport . . ."

I looked at my mother's earnest face. "Have you been talking to Gloria?" I asked her.

"What does Gloria have to do with it?"

"It's just . . . you're so . . . all of a sudden current with the research on preventable death."

My mother sagged a little. I should note that despite her poor nutritional profile, my mother has always enjoyed excellent posture. But not today. She stood in front of me, staring at her work boots, positively slumped.

It brought back thoughts of Sarah Kervick, and a sick feeling crept into my stomach. Sarah Kervick was missing. She and her father had disappeared. I thought of all the times she had protected me or Bernie, about the CD of waterfalls from around the world, of the times she tried to teach me to defend myself despite my unwavering stance as a pacifist.

I thought about how happy she'd made my mother.

"Did Gloria say . . . is there anything we can do?"

"Nope. We're not relatives. She's not technically missing."

Another pitiful whine came from the other room, and a hairy paw with nails to rival Rip Van Winkle's pushed itself beneath the door.

I grabbed the Yellow Pages from the drawer under the counter and began flipping wildly.

"He'll have to be decontaminated first," I insisted.

Under the subject heading "Pet Grooming," I skipped over the ads that marketed kindness: "Where your pets are treated like family in our home," in favor of . . .

"This is the one." I kept my finger in place and slid it over to my mother.

"The Petmeister," she read. "Flea Dips, Medicated Baths, Veterinary Supervision, Nail Trims . . . Sedatives?"

As I was reminiscing about this difficult encounter, Bernie had moved on to "salt," his other food group, and was eating a bag of pickle-and-dill potato chips. I glanced at the clock, attempting a casual tone.

"Bern? Want to hit the bathroom before we head to science?"

"No, I'm fine, Franklin. Thanks."

I studied Bernie carefully. The boy never seemed to have to go to the bathroom. I was beginning to think he was part camel. Armed with my CD and headphones, I made the long, lonely walk to the boys' bathroom by myself.

As luck would have it, Mr. Herman was just placing his wet-floor cones down when I approached.

"Mr. Herman," I said in my most respectful tone. "Would you mind . . . what I mean to say is, would it be a problem if . . ." Mr. Herman looked up at me with what might be described as a glint in his eye.

"Be my guest." As I passed his cart, I noted with approval several industrial-sized disinfecting agents. Maybe public bathrooms weren't as dangerous as I'd first thought. I was just lifting the CD player out of the specially designated zipper pocket at the top of my backpack when I thought I heard a phone ring.

"That's *my* cell," Mr. Herman said from the other side of the stall door, as if to distinguish it from all the other cells that rang in the boys' bathroom at Pelican View Middle School.

Then, to my infinite surprise, a hand reached over the door.

"It's for you."

I stood there for a moment, zipper down, staring at the phone.

"Franklin, hurry up! I only have a minute."

"Sarah?"

"Who'd you think? Of course it's me. Listen. I'm stayin' with Aunt Zinny. She is one dumb cluck, but she learned to count just so she could keep track of her cell minutes. She'll sure skin me when she finds out, but Franklin, I gotta get my skate back."

"Sarah, where are you?"

"Grand River."

"Michigan?"

"Franklin, I don't have time for this! Just listen, okay? We had to go quick, and now I'm stuck with Aunt Zinny and the brats. *You* have to bring me my skate, Franklin. I left it in the trailer. I'm still going to the regionals, so I gotta practice. It's not locked—"

"I know. I have it," I said. "But when are you coming back? My mother—"

"You have it? You *have* it? Oh man, that's a relief. But how—?"

"When we came to pick you up for pizza."

"Attaboy, Franklin!" she cheered, as if I'd just managed a bunt for Pelican View Elementary's Modern Hardware Baseball Team.

"Okay, look, I know you're in the bathroom, so you're just gonna have to memorize this. Aunt Zinny's is that blue house right at the corner of Lee and Algernon. On the West Side. They have a map at the bus station. When can you bring it?"

I'm not exactly sure why: Maybe it was the novel setting for this conversation, or perhaps the rushed and secret nature of the phone call itself, but I wasn't really catching the drift of Sarah's comments.

"I'm sure the bus won't be necessary. Grand River is just a few hours' drive. My mother—"

"Franklin, you better get this straight right now. Franklin, listen to me. I'm not asking your mom. I'm asking you. Will you bring me my skate or won't you?"

At least something about Sarah Kervick had been revived in flight. This last line was delivered in her most threatening manner.

"Look, I gotta go. I'm guessin' you're nodding your head right now. Up and down. I'll watch for you Saturday. Zinny says there's a rink near here for the hockey team, but they let kids skate after school."

"But when are you coming back? What will I tell Gloria?"

"We're gonna come back. He promised. It's just . . . he's gotta straighten out a couple things first."

"But my mother is worried sick. . . ."

"He got arrested, Franklin." Sarah exhaled sharply into the

phone. "He wasn't really doing anything wrong. It's just . . . well, he was sleeping in the backseat when his brother knocked over a 7-Eleven."

I wasn't sure how to respond to a comment like that. The backseat of a getaway car did not seem like a good place to take a nap.

As if reading my thoughts, Sarah added: "Okay, he was drunk and he passed out. Promise you won't tell your mom about that, Franklin. Not yet. I'm gonna . . . I'm gonna write her something. You'll come, right? Alone. Promise?"

What could I do? I promised, and Sarah Kervick disconnected the phone call even before I said good-bye.

I stood there, staring at the phone in my hand.

Mr. Herman's arm came over the stall door. I handed him back the telephone.

"Go on and finish up. It's almost time for the bell."

He was leaning against the porcelain fountain, a toothpick rolling across his tongue, as I emerged. He watched as I washed my hands.

"How did she know I'd be here?" I asked him.

"You're a creature of habit," he responded.

I didn't have any response to that. It was too true.

"Franklin," he said as I hurriedly applied soap for a second time and began to lather. "You ever heard of Houdini?"

I stared at Mr. Herman. A moment ago, I was in hushed conversation with Sarah Kervick in the boys'-bathroom stall, and now I was making small talk with the man who handled the lunchroom refuse.

"The magician?"

"He was that," Mr. Herman said, nodding. The bell rang, piercing the air with unsafe decibels. Mr. Herman did not flinch.

"He was also a master of escape." He pushed himself up from his leaning position by making actual contact with the rim of the urinal.

"She told me you don't like to fight. I consider that a fine thing. It's called restraint. But where you're going, you might want to at least learn a coupla hold breakers."

"Where I'm going . . . ," I repeated.

Two boys I recognized from my homeroom arrived at the door, breathless. The expressions on their faces told the whole story.

"Sorry, we . . ." They looked at each other.

"You boys go ahead," Mr. Herman said, clapping me on the shoulder and propelling me into the hall before I'd had a chance to thoroughly sanitize and dry.

"Think about it. A good hold breaker can save your skin. You don't have anything against *that*, do you?"

"Mr. Herman," I began, fighting the impulse to flinch. "Since you and Sarah are so close, I don't suppose you would consider—"

"She didn't ask me, now, did she?"

"Franklin," Bernie said, once we'd donned our safety glasses in science. "You don't look too good."

"Well, I just had a most disconcerting conversation," I said.

"With Marvin?"

"No. With Sarah Kervick."

"Go on!"

Mr. Spansky positioned himself in front of our desk and began a long discourse on protons, neutrons, and electrons.

I yanked Bernie under the table and related the high points of my conversation with Sarah. As usual, Bernie forgot himself and whacked his head on the table as I related the part about me taking Sarah's skate to Grand River.

"Didn't I say it first? I always know how the story ends!"

"Bernie, Franklin? Will you join us?" Mr. Spansky's voice came from above.

Instead of taking notes with my multicolored pen in order to highlight key concepts with efficiency, I wrote "blue house," "Lee," "Algernon," "West Side." I wondered if the West Side of Grand River was anything like the Lower East Side of New York City. I would have to research the crime statistics. I'd never actually ridden a city bus before. Would they have seat belts?

My worries were interrupted by a fine spatter of saliva on my safety glasses, and the shining, clean-shaven face of Mr. Spansky bent over to eye level with me.

"Are you listening, Mr. Donuthead? I was asking about isotopes."

# The Quest

My day was not improved by arriving home to find the shaven rear end of Zero on my favorite reading chair.

"Is the animal to be allowed on the furniture?" I called out to my mother as I shrugged off my jacket. "As a longtime resident in this home, it seems only fitting that I am consulted in these matters."

"You know what, Franklin, you are absolutely right." My mother had appeared in the doorway holding what looked like a leash and collar.

"Zero!"

Zero sat up, startled.

She looped the collar around his neck, clipped the leash to it, and handed the other end to me.

"He needs a walk," she said, helping me on with the jacket I had just removed. My arms were barely in the sleeves when she took my shoulders firmly in hand and turned me around. One rough push and I was out the front door.

"To ward off Sedentary Death Syndrome, remember?"

I looked at Zero, who had no choice but to follow me. He sat down and began scratching madly behind one ear. When he was finished, he seemed ready to go.

But where? I'd seen people trotting back and forth on the

sidewalk with their canines, but it never occurred to me to wonder about their destination. Zero gave me a mournful look. With a very close shave, courtesy of the Petmeister, he no longer looked ferocious. In fact, against the backdrop of neatly cropped lawns and manicured bushes, he looked . . . a little lost.

We stared at each other until his nose picked up a scent on the breeze. It must have been a good one, because he took off at a brisk trot, jerking so hard on my arm that dislocation seemed possible. Just when we were traveling in the same direction at the same rate of speed, he drew up sharply at a fire hydrant and began sniffing madly at the base.

I watched as Zero lifted his leg and began urinating without a care in the world. No crashing-waves CD for him! As soon as he completed this task, he was off again, following some other powerful scent. What strange creatures dogs were! He was completely ruled by his nose. It occurred to me that if I let go, Zero would soon be out of my life forever.

But then I'd have to face my mother's wrath. And—to be fair—as repellent as this canine was to me, he did hold a place in Sarah's affections. If our situations were reversed, and the potential existed for me, Franklin Delano Donuthead, to lose something I dearly valued, Sarah Kervick would hold on with a vengeance.

From there, my mind traveled to the lonely skate, now hidden under my bed, and the phone conversation I'd held earlier. I was so wrapped up in the travails of Sarah Kervick's life that I hardly noticed the peculiar expression on Zero's face just before he squatted down and defecated in dangerous proximity to the tip of my shoe.

I jumped back and pinched my nose. Zero's expression seemed now to convey: *What? Who? Me?*

To my horror, I looked up to see Mrs. Finster, the oldest living person in Pelican View, framed in her picture window, shaking a gnarled fist at me. It seemed that in order to find a soft landing spot, Zero had moved the length of the leash onto her tidy square of front lawn. I got a funny tingly feeling in my fingers and toes. Could Mrs. Finster bring suit against me for vandalizing her property? Even I, Franklin Delano Donuthead, could outrun Mrs. Finster, but there was the issue of a positive identification, and surely the evidence left behind could be linked back to us through modern DNA testing.

As I was pondering all this, Mrs. Finster opened her side door at the speed of molasses. Clutching her four-pronged cane, she bore down on me, waving a folded newspaper in her free hand.

"Franklin Donuthead. I am coming!" she called out, as if this weren't patently obvious.

"Franklin!" I turned to see Bernie charging down the sidewalk, the tails of his shirt flapping, a plastic Family Fare grocery bag ballooning at his side as it caught the breeze.

Zero, who'd been focused up to now on his creation, got all rigid and began barking furiously at Bernie, who pulled up short and thrust the bag at me.

"You better . . . pick this up . . . quick," he said, gasping for air. Out of the corner of his eye, he glimpsed Mrs. Finster. "Uh-oh."

"Young man. A word!"

Zero had stopped barking and was now scooting the very

same behind that rested in my reading chair along the heavily trafficked sidewalk.

"Were you born in a barn?" Mrs. Finster demanded, planting her cane and swaying slightly until she got her balance. Her back was so bent that she had to turn sideways and look up at us with just one eye. "The fine for failure to clean up your pet waste is five hundred dollars and a night in the county lockup. I have Sheriff Reynolds on speed dial, and if you don't— Oh hello, dear," she said, catching sight of Bernie. "Have you come to turn my Norfolk Island pine?"

Zero, too, seemed altered by the sight of Bernie. He pressed up against his side, moaning and sniffing at his pockets.

"Sure, as soon as I help Franklin clean up this mess," Bernie said, scratching Zero under the chin. Mrs. Finster sized me up and clearly, from the expression on her face, found me wanting.

"Well, as long as you have things under control, dear. I'll go get his vitamins ready. Feel free to share my methods with Mr. Donuthead here."

It did not escape me that Bernie was "dear," while I was referred to as "Mr. Donuthead."

"His vitamins?" I asked when Mrs. Finster was, at long last, out of earshot.

Bernie shrugged. "She's talking about her indoor plants. All the ivies are girls and everything else is a boy."

"And you know this because . . ."

"I guess because I turn her plants once a week."

"And you turn her plants once a week because . . ."

"Franklin, you don't have to keep pinching your nose," Bernie said. "Just breathe through your mouth. Like this . . ."

Being the ever-helpful friend, Bernie proceeded to demonstrate breathing, an activity with which I am already familiar, so I moved on to the task at hand.

"Precisely, how do you plan to get *that*," I said, pointing to Zero's creation, "into *this*?" I held up the plastic bag.

"Oh, that's easy, you just . . ." Bernie proceeded to put the bag over his hand and, to my astonishment, grab Zero's poop with it. With a quick flick, he pulled down the handles with his other hand, looped them through one another, and held the bag out to me.

I held it at arm's length, overcome with questions. Why was Mrs. Finster so fond of Bernie and so . . . disappointed with me? Why was Zero so happy to see him? Could you really earn lifelong devotion with half a dozen Thompson Treats?

Bernie, too, had his questions. He sat down on the lawn, and Zero moved in next to him, laying his big mangy head in Bernie's lap.

"I just keep thinking about Sarah and if she's ever comin' back. Do you think so?" He sighed. "I guess we'll know more after you bring her the skate," Bernie mused, getting that far-away look in his eyes. "Are you sure you're ready for this, Franklin? Sarah's going to be so surprised. . . ."

I looked hard at Bernie. He really did live in a fantasy world. Wasn't he here to witness that I, Franklin Delano Donuthead, could not even effectively pick up dog poop? How, then, was I supposed to travel to Grand River, the eighth-largest metropolis in the Midwest, to deliver a "package"? With my luck, I would be arrested on suspicion of drug trafficking.

I sighed, too, and sat down next to Bernie. What was it Gloria said?

*Everything's not changing, Franklin, you are.*

Me. Franklin Delano Donuthead. On a quest.

"I hope I'm ready," I said to Bernie, and forced myself not to pull away as he patted me on the back with the same hand that had maneuvered Zero's poop.

# The Rules Meant to Be Broken

The next day, I sat in health class, ordering my notes on the forms of healthy love. Though I'd studied in my usual manner—making outlines and index cards—the information was not sticking. I kept getting confused! A test appeared on my desk, and I leaned instinctively into the aisle to remind Sarah Kervick to put her name on her paper. Suddenly I was overcome with memories that placed a higher demand on my attention than filling out the multiple-choice section on how to be a respectful listener.

I saw the look on Sarah Kervick's face just before she tried to put her fist in her mouth to stop the happiness from leaking out when Gloria sent her the ice skates from Washington, D.C. Then I thought of my mother hollering from the stands the day I made a single for the Modern Hardware Baseball Team. And Sarah throwing her hands in the air after she landed her first single lutz.

Ten Vermilion Sunset fingernails appeared suddenly on my blank test paper.

"Franklin?" Miss Mathews bent close and whispered to me. "Can I ask you something? I haven't seen Sarah since her skating show, and nobody ever answers the phone number we have in our records. Do you know how I can get in touch with her?"

The combination of her breath on my ear and the sight of her collarbone, which was suddenly in plain view, set off a diversion of blood flow so severe I was afraid my heart would stop.

"I don't," I said, keeping my eyes on my test paper.

"She's been absent so many days that I'm going to have to report her to the truant officer."

I forced myself to look at Miss Mathews, whose face was registering genuine concern. "I don't want to get her in trouble, Franklin. I just need her to come to class. Do you think you could talk to her?"

I swallowed. "I don't think she's absent," I whispered. "I think she's . . . moved."

"Oh . . . I'm sorry." Miss Mathews stood up. "And I'm keeping you from your test. I don't want to ruin your A-plus record."

As I turned back to my test paper, I caught sight of one Marvin Howerton, his eyebrows raised in mock surprise.

"Donut-dork," he whispered. "You lost your bodyguard."

I could only imagine the sort of ancient Chinese torture devices he'd be ordering through the mail to practice on me in Sarah's absence.

At the lunch table, Bernie Lepner, my new travel agent, was helping to plan my itinerary.

"A lot of people take the bus to Grand River, Franklin. My aunt and uncle go every year the day after Thanksgiving to see the Christmas display in the store windows at Herpolsheimer's."

"Why don't they drive?"

"Well, it costs seventeen dollars to park all day. That doesn't include the gas."

Though I hadn't spent much time around Bernie's aunt and uncle, they seemed like orderly, law-abiding people. Perhaps the mass-transit system was filled with elderly types on fixed incomes and not—as I feared—gang members and winos.

"The bus picks up in the parking lot behind Perkins' Drug Store. There's only one time in the morning and one time at night. You can buy your ticket ahead of time at the post office."

"I'll be arriving back at night?" I said, my mind rushing to the correlation between darkness and personal-assault injuries.

This was followed by a long silence as Bernie and I retreated into our own separate fantasies. As we were gathering our things in anticipation of the bell, he said: "Do you want me to take you to the bathroom, Franklin?"

I paused to let the full meaning of what Bernie had just said sink in. Here he was—a ten-year-old, for Pete's sake—offering to take me to the bathroom because the person who usually escorted me—a girl!—was no longer available. While I appreciated the gesture, even I could see this placed me squarely in the pathetic category. Franklin Delano Roosevelt must be turning over in his grave.

"I'm leaving on Saturday, Bernie. Alone."

Bernie stood up, a small piece of ramen noodle stuck to his chin.

"Really?"

"Yes, really. Alone," I repeated, just to make sure I'd heard it right.

Throwing caution to the wind, I decided to exit the cafeteria via the double doors on the opposite side of the room, bringing me within feet of the fair Ms. Powell.

On my way there, however, I spied Marvin Howerton moving toward me with purposefully evil intent. Given the rate at which he was traveling, I predicted we would meet just short of the end of the last long lunch table, Marvin's purpose being to employ one of the laws of physics to transfer his energy *through* me to the table, causing its contents to fly through the air and implicate me in a crime I did not commit. In hockey terminology, this is known as a "body check."

Instead of scurrying in the other direction—as was my custom—I continued at a fixed rate of speed toward our collision, stopping abruptly one second short of impact.

Marvin sprawled across the lunch table, drawing the attention of Mr. Fiegel, who flicked on his bullhorn and barked: "Howerton! Lunch duty!"

"Me!? I didn't do anything! It was Donut-dork who made me do it."

"Name calling is a penalty, Mr. Howerton. That will be *two* lunch duties for you," Mr. Fiegel said.

I walked the empty halls, safe in the knowledge that Marvin Howerton was being detained to gather lunch trays. A momentary sense of well-being filled me. Maybe, I thought, entering the bathroom, just maybe I could take care of myself.

But then I almost got nailed by Mr. Herman as he went through his paces.

"Franklin," he said, pulling up short. There was a film of sweat on his face. Apparently, swinging a broomstick to ward off imaginary opponents was a good cardiovascular activity.

"You probably shouldn't surprise me like that."

My plan had been to proceed confidently to the fountain

and unzip, but Mr. Herman's broom handle had drained the confidence right out of me.

"Mr. Herman," I said, blinking. "Would you consider teaching me a few of those evasive moves you described yesterday?"

Mr. Herman screwed the handle into the broom and leaned on it, staring at me intently.

"When are you leaving?"

"Day after tomorrow."

He pressed his lips together, thinking. "Okay." He placed his feet shoulder width apart, in much the same way Sarah Kervick did when preparing to give me one of the "life lessons" that I would routinely ignore.

"Now, if you are close enough to touch someone on the ear . . . ," he said, reaching out and touching mine, "you are close enough to gouge someone's eye out." He then placed his thumb over my closed left eye and pressed down, demonstrating.

"Mr. Herman," I said. "You should know that the only thing I can do violently is tremble. I am, at heart, a peaceful boy."

"Okay, how about this little jab right here? Keep your fingers rigid . . ."

He demonstrated some sort of ninja stealth maneuver involving two stiffened fingers in a trajectory to the windpipe. Mr. Herman did not leave much to the imagination. I was beginning to see why he and Sarah Kervick got along so famously.

I cleared my throat. "Mr. Herman, I was under the impression that you would teach me ways to safely escape an attacker, not maim one. I am a pacifist, Mr. Herman. In the words of the late, great Franklin Delano Roosevelt . . ."

"Didn't he get us into war after Pearl Harbor?" Mr. Herman

asked me. "Seems to me, there are times when a little fight is the only reasonable alternative. Listen, son, I always teach my students to walk away, but when someone wants to attack you, a bunch of words from a dead president won't save you from the emergency room. Your job is to disable him—not permanently, but long enough to escape. One quick move like this . . ."

Mr. Herman demonstrated yet another move, which constituted jabbing the heel of his hand toward my face and stopping just short of my nose.

". . . lets you walk away. Face it, Franklin. You're a shrimp. Shrimps need to rely on the element of surprise."

"A shrimp," I replied indignantly, "is a bottom-feeding crustacean whose only natural defense is a tough outer shell."

"Then you better grow one before Saturday, 'cause Sarah Kervick isn't staying at the Ritz."

I sighed heavily. Were there no realistic options for the peaceful among us?

Just to show there were no hard feelings, Mr. Herman patted me on the shoulder.

Unable to resist one more little demonstration, he fingered the tendons between my shoulder and my neck. "If you pinch right here . . ."

The horrified look on my face must have stopped him.

"Well, I'll leave you alone to do your business."

For that, I was truly thankful. "Thank you, Mr. Herman," I said, concealing myself behind the stall door and trying to sound grateful, because I knew he meant well.

I was so distracted by the sound of the first bell, and the imagined injuries Mr. Herman might inflict if he followed through with one of his disabling tactics, that once I was inside the stall, my plumbing worked quite efficiently. Even without the CD.

"Gone? Just vanished?" Mrs. Boardman had finished shaking my hand, but she held on anyway.

"I'm afraid so."

"But the nonfiction . . . we, I . . . I brought her a book from the library over in Wing Rock."

"It's all very sudden," I agreed. I led Mrs. Boardman over to her chair and asked if she wanted a glass of water. Mrs. Boardman nodded yes and, after she'd taken a few sips, looked up at me over the rims of her bifocals.

"You will find her, won't you Franklin?"

"I'm going to try."

"You're a nice boy." She patted my hand.

Part of me wanted to tell Mrs. Boardman about my plan to head to Grand River, but I felt that a person her age might be bound to inform my mother. And then where would I be?

"I will admit that I'm a tad worried about the trying part."

I stood at the reshelving cart, sorting the books into categories: picture books, fiction, biography, world religions.

"Worried?"

"Well, I'm afraid I'll get myself into a situation . . . I might encounter a bully or get lost. I'm not sure what I'll do if I get lost. . . . In stories, there always seems to be something magic, like a ball of yarn or seven-league boots or a talking apple. But this is not a folktale, Mrs. Boardman."

" 'There is no living thing that is not afraid when it faces danger,' Franklin dear. 'True courage is in facing danger when you are afraid.' Do you know who said that?"

I shook my head. It sounded familiar, but I couldn't place it.

"It comes from *The Wizard of Oz,* and it's what the wizard said to the cowardly lion."

We began with the sciences. Mrs. Boardman inserted the ruler, and I followed with the correct book according to the Dewey decimal system. Then she handed me the picture books in alphabetical order as I shelved them on my knees. It felt good to put things in order. That's what librarians do, when you think about it. They put the world back into order, one book at a time.

As soon as I got home, I placed a call to Gloria, planning to casually draw out of her the Grand River, Michigan, block-by-block crime statistics. But Miss Tweedell answered her phone.

"Oh hello, Franklin. Gloria's not here today. She's at the annual AURA meeting in Chicago."

"The *aura* meeting?"

"American Union of Risk Analysts."

This was most unsettling. "How long will she be gone?"

"I think . . . checking her schedule . . . until Monday, dear. Do you want her voice mail?"

"No thank you. I'll just . . . well, hope you hear from me on Monday."

"All righty, then. Have a good weekend, Franklin. Don't do anything I wouldn't do, hear?"

If Miss Tweedell only knew.

CHAPTER SIXTEEN

# Bursting My Antibacterial Soap Bubble

With the exception of certain statements I have made regarding the enjoyment of attending baseball games, I have never told my mother a falsehood. Lying is a quality that does not keep company with principles such as health promotion and mental improvement. I have employed this tactic on occasion, with Marvin Howerton, to aid in risk avoidance.

For example, if Marvin were to say: "Hey, Donuthead, you goin' to the john?" I might reply something like: "Actually, I was . . . on my way to the office to check my community-service hours."

Or:

"Hey, Donut-hole, wanna walk home with us?"

"That'd be great, Marvin, but . . . I just remembered I promised Mr. Spansky I would sanitize the petri dishes."

Since Marvin was not sincere in his interest, it was easy to lie to him. My mother, on the other hand, would be a different story.

On Friday evening, Paul was over—yet again—under the pretense of helping my mother pick out new paint colors for the living room. Since Sarah Kervick had disappeared, my mother had thrown herself into redecorating the house with intense energy. Helping my mother make decisions about our home decor used to be my job. That was all before Paul, HGTV on cable, and home-dec-in-a-sec parties in our neighborhood. Still, I tried to maintain a small but meaningful role by slipping in the flyer I'd requested on milk-based paints in classic colonial colors.

As I sat upstairs, getting my story straight, I heard Paul say: "What's this? Looks like fourteen shades of mud."

"Oh, that's Franklin's idea. It's milk paint. No volatile organic compounds."

"Huh?"

"There's no outgassing."

"Get him down here. I'll show him outgassing."

"Paul!"

You might think a comment like that would have stayed my progress, but no, I remained determined. As I crept downstairs, I noticed that my mother had given Zero one of the rawhide bones she'd purchased at Chow Hound. Rawhide is a nice word for "dehydrated skin of a dead cow." Shards of saliva-soaked rawhide were now sprinkled across our carpet.

*Must not run for vacuum with HEPA filter. Must stay focused.*

"Mother," I managed to say, holding tight to the banister. "I intend to be with Bernie all day Saturday. We're going to the library to get information for our database, then, um, lunch at Perkins' Drug Store, followed by . . . a trip to Van Hoek's. Bernie needs new tennis shoes and, well, he's requested my presence to evaluate the footwear for durability and safety. Following that . . ."

"You'll be gone with Bernie all day?"

I braced myself for the interrogation to follow.

"Okay." My mother grabbed Paul's arm. "Hey, we can go to that countertop-and-tile place in Conklin."

Paul took this opportunity to put his face in my mother's hair. "I hear they're doing karaoke at the Whistle Stop now."

My mother peeled a few bills from her money clip and held them out to me.

"Lunch is on me. Perkins' Drug Store, eh? Don't eat too many cinnamon rolls, Franklin. You know, too much sugar isn't good for you."

Though Paul laughed heartily, I thought this a very lame joke. So much for an interrogation of my movements. She was happy to be rid of me. I wonder what she would think if she knew I was boarding a Transit Authority bus bound for the bowels of the city.

*This is not where they listen to the carillon chimes by the town square,* a less mature Franklin might have shouted at her. *This is the 'hood, Mother. Think feral dogs, rusty nails. I might even see a discarded needle that was once used to inject drugs.*

The very thought sent me rushing back upstairs to double-check my vaccination record.

Back in my room, I pulled out Sarah's backpack and began to empty it of all but the figure skate and the teddy bear, reasoning that there was no need to take her school folders to Grand River. Though they had a generally crumpled appearance—one even bore a bicycle tire tread!—the folders obviously hadn't seen much use.

I was surprised to see my own name on her health folder.

"Tell Franklin!" she'd written and underlined several times. I opened the folder to find it stuffed with—not handouts and notes on healthy vs. unhealthy love or the toxicity of cigarettes—past-due bills and notices of cancellation of service.

*Tell Franklin!*

Sarah Kervick had almost confided in me. She'd actually believed, at least for a moment, that I could help her out of her difficulties. I sat on my bed and looked over her possessions. I was beginning to feel a bit, well, petrified about what I was about to do.

I couldn't help it. It was late on Friday. She wasn't in the office and there was nothing she could do, but I wanted to hear Gloria's voice before I departed. After two quick rings, her machine began:

"This is Gloria Nelots. Did you know that 85 percent of the people who drowned in boating-related accidents last year were not wearing life jackets? If you're heading out for a boat ride, for heaven's sake, buckle into a life preserver. Oh, and check for power lines before launching. Now leave me a safe message, and I'll get back to you as soon as I can."

*Beep.*

"Gloria? This is Franklin. You won't get this until you return, but I think you should know I have located Sarah Kervick and I am going to, uh, visit her tomorrow . . . that is, Saturday. I hope I make it back okay. I was just calling to ask you about something, but . . . I guess I would go even if Grand River did have shocking crime statistics. Because I promised that I would. And because, well, I bet William would have gone. I mean, if he knew Sarah Kervick. Even if he was only eleven and three-quarters years old . . ." I sighed. "Well, that's all for now, Gloria. . . . All right, then. Good-bye."

• • •

The next morning, after I purchased my ticket at the post office, I had just one more errand to run before setting off for Grand River. It was something I'd been thinking about for days. Though the ticket had been covered by my allowance, I had to raid the envelope with the remainder of my birthday money for this one.

Fields' Flowers was located on Main Street two doors down from the post office. It was run by a Mr. Tranh, who came to America as a young man. Our local paper, *The Pelican View,* had just done a big write-up on his becoming an American citizen. Certainly, no one was more careful with his American flag than Mr. Tranh, who took it down at the end of each business day in the official manner set forth by the United States Code.

I entered Mr. Tranh's shop. It was cool and dark and smelled pleasantly of green growing things. Mr. Tranh was behind the counter near the cooler.

"Good morning," I said. "I would like to buy some flowers."

Without looking up, Mr. Tranh studied the index card on which I'd copied Gloria's address. "Ah, yes," he said. "Washington, D.C. We send them FTD."

Mr. Tranh pulled out a book with thick plastic pages and began flipping through them.

"Anniversary? Wedding?"

"No. Birthday." I tried to focus on all the possibilities, but Mr. Tranh was flipping very quickly.

"Oh, lovely. Birthday." He began paging in a different direction. "How old?"

"Well, he would have been fifty-seven."

Mr. Tranh tore a piece of paper from a thick pad next to the cash register. An official FTD form. I began to fill it out, hoping thirty-five dollars was enough to buy something in this book.

"Yes, yes. How old is he now?"

"Uh, he's dead."

Mr. Tranh looked at me as if his understanding of English had failed him. "Birthday flowers to dead person? No, no. Sympathy."

This required another book altogether. I looked over the bouquets appropriate for when someone died. Lots of white lilies and silver. They didn't seem right. Gloria had said William was like Sarah. I pictured him on the ball field, weaving between the other players, narrowly avoiding disaster. Like she was, full of energy.

"No." I shook my head firmly to make sure Mr. Tranh understood. "Happy flowers. Happy birthday. He is fifty-seven next week."

Mr. Tranh sighed and repositioned his glasses. He seemed to think he would be held personally responsible for sending the wrong kind of flowers across the nation. He put the sympathy book away and slowly flipped through the "Happy Birthday" section again.

"Message?" he asked, pointing to a box on the form. "We type. It go through computer, come out in Washington, D.C."

"I want to use this poem." I passed the poem over to

Mr. Tranh. To remember William, I had chosen "Passing Love" by Langston Hughes—over the years I'd learned Gloria was a big fan of his poetry.

> *Because you are to me a song*
> *I must not sing you over-long.*
>
> *Because you are to me a prayer*
> *I cannot say you everywhere.*
>
> *Because you are to me a rose—*
> *You will not stay when summer goes.*

I tried to wait patiently as Mr. Tranh copied the poem into the message box.

When he was finished, he said, "From . . ."

"Do I have to say who it's from? Can't we just have the poem?"

He shook his head vigorously. "Always say. Always sign card. Creepy for Gloria to get flowers from no one. Especially for dead person on her birthday."

"But it's not *her* birthday. It's his. Her brother's. Her brother died in Vietnam."

Mr. Tranh stopped short. His eyes got bigger. "Aah, I see. This is very special. Fallen soldier. Memorial flowers." He paged furiously to a veritable riot of red, white, and blue. "We use special ribbon, with stars."

I almost didn't have the energy to fight with him. He

seemed so anxious to help, but these red carnations and white roses just weren't right.

"I'm sorry, Mr. Tranh, but I need a different kind of flowers. Don't you have anything . . . wild . . . and restless?"

Mr. Tranh kneaded his face in his hands. He pulled yet another book from under the counter and paged through it. He smoothed the pages and turned the book around.

"Yes," I said. "That's it!" Wildflowers spilled out of the vase in no particular order. Big purple sprays and clusters of orange. Long blue tubes of color. Not my taste, exactly. But just right all the same.

"I hope I have enough," I said as Mr. Tranh tapped energetically on the cash register.

"How much you have?" he asked.

"Thirty-five dollars."

He stopped tapping. "We do it without vase. Nice bow. Thirty-five dollars. Even."

The bell behind me jingled, and another customer walked in. "Aah, here come my best customer. Mr. Bernard come in every day to get rose for his sweetheart."

"Hey, Franklin. I'm just on my way to your house. Getting a little something for Glynnis?"

My news traveled fast. I faced Paul, who looked tidier than usual in a blue-checked plaid shirt tucked in at the waist. For some reason, I was unable to compose a reasonable answer. Had I just blown my cover by being seen in the flower shop? What exactly had I told my mother I'd be doing at this hour? Come to think of it, if Paul bought a rose for my mother every day, what happened to all those flowers? Did she throw them out? Hide them?

"Gloria" was the only word I could manage.

"Gloria?"

I held out the FTD form. "To remember her brother. He would have been fifty-seven."

Paul read over the form. "Can I see?" he asked, picking up the book with the bouquet.

"A Vietnam veteran," Mr. Tranh said. "Very special memorial flowers." Obviously Mr. Tranh did not have to take the kind of privacy oaths that lawyers and doctors did.

"Well, you're going to put a rose in there, aren't you? It's got a rose right in the poem."

"I'm afraid that would be over my budget."

"I will add red rose to bouquet," Mr. Tranh announced expansively, "to honor American hero."

"No need for that, Anh Dung," Paul said, pulling bills from his wallet. "Just add it to my tab today. And give me one of those French beauties you got in the back."

As Mr. Tranh disappeared into the cooler, Paul said: "So, Franklin, I thought you were allergic to flowers."

"Well, some varieties do cause mild sensations of itching—"

"I just assumed that's why your mom always kept hers in the van."

"I—"

"But now that I know you're a flower man, like myself, well . . . you know, Franklin, I've been thinking . . ." Paul leaned up against the counter as if he was warming up to say something. It was most disconcerting.

"We should spend a little time together, you and me. . . . You know . . ." He scratched his chest, thinking. "Uh . . . maybe pick up some health food and . . . I don't know. Hit the museum?"

Mr. Tranh had returned with a single apricot-colored rose. He sprayed it with a fine mist and held it up for Paul's inspection. Paul nodded his approval.

"Tissue color?" Mr. Tranh asked.

Paul thought for a moment. "Dark gray," he said. "So what do you say, Franklin? You and me?"

I glanced at my watch. It was almost time for my scheduled departure. I placed my money on the counter and began backing toward the door. "Sounds good," I said, attempting a casual tone. "See you around, Paul."

I hurried to the parking lot behind Perkins' Drug Store, clutching my bus ticket in my sweaty palm. Sarah's skate kept whacking me on the back. The thought occurred to me that if my bag was searched, the skate could be considered a lethal weapon. Weapons of any kind were strictly prohibited on any Transit Authority bus.

For the sake of convenience, I'd memorized the lengthy code of "Riding Rules." It would be easy to refrain from using alcohol or other illegal substances; using obscene, threatening, inciting, or insulting language or gestures; spitting, littering, or picking trash from receptacles; vandalizing; fighting, mock fighting, or roughhousing; standing, sitting, or walking in a way that inconveniences other passengers; loitering, panhandling, or soliciting; or using a radio, CD player, or other sound-producing device without headphones.

But if Gammy Donuthead could have her knitting needles

confiscated on her most recent flight to Florida, could not Sarah Kervick's recently sharpened skate be cause for concern?

I was thinking I would just have to risk it when I saw—as if in a dream—Glynnis Powell running toward me across the asphalt. She was wearing a loose-fitting pair of slacks with a belted cardigan. One hand kept a beret atop her head. I squinted. Could it be a mirage? No, there was Bernie Lepner, bringing up the rear and trying to hold on to an enormous German shepherd clad in two canvas bags and a harness.

"Franklin!" Glynnis came to a stop directly in front of me, looking quite disheveled. She pressed a hand to her heart. With the other, she straightened her little hat and combed a few loose hairs behind her ear.

"I . . ." But she was too out of breath to continue.

"We made it!" Bernie had managed to keep hold of the animal that now sat, barely winded, and gazed up at Glynnis with adoration. The lettering on his harness read: PAWS WITH A PURPOSE. I AM IN TRAINING.

"Franklin, I . . ." Her eyes met mine and she faltered again. Only this time, she wasn't out of breath. I saw her perfect mouth form a little O of embarrassment, and she blushed deeply.

"I told Glynnis where you were going, and she wanted to help," Bernie said.

Glynnis put her hand on the dog's head. "I brought you Bartleby," she said.

"Bartleby?" I repeated. "As in . . ."

Glynnis smiled and looked at the ground. "The Scrivener."

I sighed. Hardly anybody our age reads Melville. Glynnis really was a reader.

"Is he . . . yours?" Somehow, I'd never pictured Glynnis with a dog before. She seemed too . . . well, too neat.

She nodded again. "My stepfather is Trevor Thompson."

"He's the one on TV," Bernie said, oh so helpfully. "You know, Thompson Treats, TrevorTime dog and cat food, T & T Hairball Remover . . ."

"I'm familiar with the product line, Bernie," I replied, hoping to silence him. I wanted just a moment to absorb the scene in front of me, zooming in on Glynnis and cropping Bernie and the dog from the picture.

"Your real father?" I asked her.

"My parents are divorced."

"Is it strange . . . ? I mean, I might be getting a stepfather . . . someday."

"It's a little strange," she said. Her gaze had come up to my chest. She combed the same hair behind her ears. "Well . . ." She exhaled sharply. "A lot strange if you really want to know."

"Here's the bus!" Bernie shouted, far louder than was necessary.

"Oh!" Glynnis seemed to recall why she had come in the first place. "He's not really in training. He's a personal-protection dog. But they let dogs go on the bus like this. Just hang on to the handles, Franklin, and he'll protect you."

"Oh, I don't think a dog—"

"It's a jungle out there, Franklin," Bernie said. "Two years ago, my aunt and uncle got their disability check stolen."

"I guess you neglected to tell me *that*, didn't you?"

The bus door whooshed open.

Glynnis kneeled down in front of the dog. She put her hands on his ears and stroked them.

"Say good-bye, Barty."

What I saw next pains me even to repeat. Glynnis allowed that dog—that dog whose mouth may have come into contact with toilet water, its own reproductive organs, even day-old Dumpster trash—to lick her on the mouth.

I took a step back in shock. I felt sick to my stomach.

She leaned forward to whisper: "Unless you're in hot water, don't say the state motto. It's his signal to attack. Good luck, Franklin."

"Need some help there?" the driver shouted. "We're on a schedule, pal."

Still incredulous, I took the handle on the dog's harness and pulled slightly. Bartleby's head swiveled back and forth between me and Glynnis. Her eyes were on him, urging him forward. She made a gesture with her hand.

I didn't know dogs could sigh. But Bartleby let out a long one before trotting up the steps with me.

"Handi-dogs in front," the driver said. She was what the weight charts call "morbidly obese," with iron-gray hair that didn't quite cover her head. And she was chewing gum. With her mouth open.

I sat down in the front row of seats, the ones that face each other rather than forward. HANDICAPPED ACCESSIBLE, the sign read. SECUREMENTS AVAILABLE BENEATH THE BENCH. Bartleby and I looked at each other for a long moment before he chose a spot half under and half extending out into the aisle. This would clearly be a problem, as it blocked the aisle for future passengers. I knew what would make him attack—the state motto. I knew various other dog words, such as *come, sit,* and *stay*. But I did not know how to communicate: *Can you please scoot back a little so you're not blocking the aisle?*

The bus lurched to life, and I looked out the window at Glynnis and Bernie, standing side by side, waving at the retreating bus. I could not shake the image of Bartleby licking Glynnis. Talk about bursting my Ivory-soap bubble. The distressing thought occurred to me that there might be other things about Glynnis that—when I discovered them—would tarnish my image of her perfection.

And yet, there were Glynnis and Bernie, growing smaller by the moment. What would they do now? I wondered. Go over our geography assignment? Conjugate a few Spanish verbs? Whatever pleasant activities their day held, my course was set. I was heading for Grand River, the eighth largest metropolis in the Midwest, heading to the heart of the city, to deliver one figure skate to its rightful owner.

CHAPTER SEVENTEEN

# Saved by a Pleasant Peninsula

The ride from Pelican View to the outskirts of the city was, for the most part, uneventful. I attempted to get the bus driver to share the secret of the securements. . . . Were these actually seat belts? I asked her politely.

"We use those for the paralytics," she told me.

"So I shouldn't—"

"Not unless you're a paralytic."

Bartleby, it seemed, shared Mr. Spansky's deficiency in being able to contain saliva in his mouth. I found it necessary to shift my feet around in a regular pattern to avoid the spot directly beneath his muzzle. The bus driver, whose open mouth I glimpsed regularly in the rearview mirror, seemed to alternate between blowing her nose and getting the heavy-lidded expression that comes before falling asleep.

After what seemed like many hours, but was actually two hours and forty-seven minutes, we arrived from the west, cresting the hill and viewing the cityscape spread out below us. The rolling curve of the central bus depot was part of the skyline. I'd seen this exact view on the Web site. The occasional field and neatly clipped expanse of lawn gave way to brick and clapboard houses and storefronts pushed together in haphazard confusion.

As we drove closer to the heart of town, the city's unfortunates seemed magnetically attracted to our bus. A hefty sort with a bulging belly and a daisy chain made out of neckties boarded the bus and dropped his coins into the change meter.

Instead of proceeding in an orderly fashion down the aisle, he stopped in front of me, scratching his belly, and sat down across from us.

"I'm thinking if Jesus wore pants, he'd put them on one leg at a time," he said. "What's your opinion?"

"I have no opinion," I said, pushing up against the back of my seat.

"Fillmore Avenue and Gentian," the bus driver called.

"Everybody's got an opinion," he said, fumbling in his shirt pocket for a pack of gum. "Leastwise, everybody's got an opinion about Jesus. . . ."

This fascinating conversation was interrupted by yet another stop. Several people in business attire boarded the bus. A teenager who did not have the benefit of the "flour baby" assignment lugged a car seat holding an infant to the back. A hoodlum with a pair of headphones and a pierced nose shuffled to the first seat in the "regular" row. Bartleby strained to give him an olfactory inspection.

I tugged on his harness. "You're in training, remember?"

He made a noise that sounded like a growl, reminding me that while he might seem to the world to be a "handi-dog," he was really a vicious personal-protection dog on loan from Glynnis. A dog that attacked upon hearing our state motto. What *was* our state motto anyway? *Looking all around you . . .*

No, that wasn't it. *If you're looking for a pleasant state . . .* I knew it had something to do with geography. How effective was a protection dog if I didn't even know the order for attack?

Not that my lifelong principles of pacifism would allow me to use such an order. But it would be a comfort to know it.

An old woman had boarded the bus and was rummaging through her crochet bag for her bus pass.

"I know it's here," she said, taking the closest seat to the driver. "Lily will just have a peek." She continued searching. I noticed that hair sprouted from underneath her chin. Abandoning the search in her purse, Lily took advantage of the moment the bus driver leaned over to adjust the side-view mirror to reach out and snatch a paper soft-drink cup from the garbage. This was a clear violation of the riding rules. Lily sucked on the straw, extracting the last of the liquid.

"Cherry Coke," she said. "My favorite."

I now know it is not possible to die from being in the presence of disgusting behavior, because I am still alive.

All Transit Authority buses begin and end at the central bus depot, just south of Plimpton on Main. As our bus pulled in, the able-bodied among us rose in their seats. Bartleby looked up at me. The bus stopped with a hiss.

"Come," I said. It worked. Bartleby got to his feet.

"Central depot!" the bus driver shouted before heaving herself to a standing position. She was off the bus before most of the customers, which did not seem at all like proper procedure. Without the driver present, Lily began rummaging through the garbage in earnest.

I realized that soon, I would have to board another bus and

be exposed to yet another set of questionable characters. It made me tired just thinking about it.

Bartleby and I enjoyed a quick walk around the concrete deck of the bus depot. It occurred to me that he might have to "do his business." I glanced around for a likely spot and, finding no grass in the vicinity, took him over to a couple of bushes surrounded by gravel.

"Here, boy," I said, pointing to the bush and trying to concoct an interspecies sign to indicate that going to the bathroom was acceptable. Bartleby cocked his head and looked up at me. I continued my ridiculous pantomime until the driver once again appeared from the depot. If Bartleby was going to do something, it would have to be fast. I towed him inside and went up to the information booth.

"Excuse me," I said to the woman behind the counter. "Do you have a dog-relief area in the vicinity?"

She looked at me as if no one had ever asked this question before. Then she slid open the window that separated us and leaned out over the counter to get a look at Bartleby. He rewarded her with a friendly bark.

"You're supposed to bring your own pad. You know that," she said severely, and lowered the window once again.

My own pad? Whatever could she be talking about? Some sort of canine diaper? I looked at Bartleby, who did not seem to be suffering any discomfort. I shrugged. *Welcome to my world, boy.*

Back on the deck, I quickly located the Number 13 Staunton Westbound.

*Come* still worked its magic, and Bartleby and I were soon

aboard our last bus. I inserted a dollar fifty into the fare box and received my ticket.

Somehow, we made it to the corner of Penzey and Algernon, and the bus left us in a cloud of exhaust. I looked around. This was not the sort of place I would frequently inhabit, and yet it didn't have the deserted, back-alley flavor I'd feared. People obviously lived and worked here. Kids rode their bicycles. I drew my coat around me, took a deep breath, and told myself to attend to the business at hand.

I'd been let out at Mike's Party Store. Several youth burst out with sodas and bags of jalapeño Cheetos and streamed around us, leaving a respectful space for Bartleby. I patted him on the head. Glynnis was right. Despite my natural aversion to animals, it was comforting to have Bartleby along.

We headed north as per the map I'd consulted on the bus. The cross streets had creative names like Summer and Winter. Having exhausted the seasons, we moved on to flowers. I'd crossed Pansy, Daffodil, and Trillium when I began to wonder how much farther we had to go. The map at the bus station did not make the trip seem so far. Surely, another city bus route would have been indicated if this was the case.

At least, Bartleby didn't mind. He trotted along beside me quite happily, though I did notice that between Trillium and Poppy his tongue began dangling from his mouth. Was he overheating? Thirsty?

"Hey, what's this?" A gangly boy in jeans and an extra-large T-shirt launched himself over the porch railing of a house that could only be described as a fixer-upper. He whistled through his teeth, and two other boys appeared in the doorway.

"Scrub, this is one them handi-dogs I was telling you about."

Scrub, who was shorter and thicker than the first boy, kneeled down in front of Bartleby and scratched under his chin. Bartleby sat down and tilted his head upward. Obviously, he was hoping to stay awhile.

"What can he do?" Scrub asked me.

"Well, uh . . . he's just in training, as you can see. . . ." I cast around for something that sounded authentic. "By the time we're through with him, he'll be able to . . . turn off light switches, fetch the telephone, and, um . . . press the buttons on the microwave with his nose. Say, would you gentlemen know where I can find Lee Street?"

A third boy pulled on a sweat jacket and lumbered down the stairs toward us.

"'Bout two miles that way, I'd say. Can I pet your dog, too?"

"Well, you're not supposed to pet the dog while he's in training, actually."

Bartleby was now letting all the boys scratch his side.

"Hey, this would be a great dog for Granddad, Pete," the tall boy said. He looked up at me. "Our granddad had a stroke. Now he can't move on one side."

"Well, those are the kind of people we're looking for," I said, trying to be friendly. The boys were on all sides of us now, and I started to get that tingly feeling in my fingers and toes, the one that signals either danger or Miss Mathews in a sundress. "But there's quite a waiting list down at the handicapped training center."

The first boy had now moved to Bartleby's ears. Pete was

rubbing his hindquarters. The dog seemed to enjoy this very much. I wondered if he would change allegiances for some boys with a good scratching technique.

"Nick. Let's take him inside and show Granddad."

"Good idea," Nick said. "That'll cheer him up. Hey, kid, wanna go inside?"

I most certainly did not. Going into the homes of strangers was strictly limited to characters in books. Hansel and Gretel come to mind. And look where it got them! I cast around for some assistance. I was beginning to feel a bit claustrophobic. The street appeared to be empty. Perhaps Bartleby and I could make a dash for Mike's Party Store. But then, for all I knew, these boys held him up on weekends. I heard a car turn the corner. If I threw myself into the street . . .

"C'mon," Nick said, growing impatient. He began to tug at Bartleby's harness. "It'll cheer him up. Just for a minute."

Mr. Herman's techniques flashed through my mind, but how could I push the heel of my hand into Nick's nose when I couldn't even reach it. And he was just one of this pack. We hadn't covered multiple attackers! I tried to remain calm. We weren't being attacked. We were on a public sidewalk. All we had to do was walk away and things would be fine.

"Here, pup." Scrub stood up, too, and snapped his fingers.

Bartleby stood up, looking first at me, then at the other boys. He took a step in their direction. All they really wanted was the dog, I told myself, before taking a giant step backward.

*What was I thinking? This was Glynnis' beloved pet!*

Mr. Herman was right. I was a shrimp, one who'd neglected to grow a hard outer shell. There is a moment—I can say this now with some authority—when you are cornered, the jig is up, your time is cut short. At this moment, you are—at first—completely drained of thought. But then one idea floats up to you through the numbing darkness: one card to play, one last roll of the dice, so to speak.

"Franklin Delano Roosevelt."

"Huh?"

Of course. My namesake. What matter that he'd been dead for half a century? Standing in front of these boys, hopelessly outnumbered, I felt the words from FDR's inspirational speeches flow through me: *There are many ways of going forward, but only one way of standing still.* And *It isn't sufficient just to want—you've got to ask yourself what you are going to do to get the things you want.* And *We cannot always build the future for our youth, but we can build our youth for the future.* And even *There is nothing I love as much as a good fight.*

I was like a boy possessed. The words of FDR poured into me like spinach from Popeye's can. I swear I felt myself transforming into our late, great president—before his wheelchair days, of course.

"Will ya look at that? He's twitching." Scrub took a step backward.

"Step aside, Scrub, Nicholas," I said. "And remember, you are just an extra in everyone else's play."

"What?"

"I do not believe in communism any more than you do, but there is nothing wrong with communists in this country."

"He's just *trying* to act crazy so we leave him alone," Nick said. "Have at it, kid. It's the dog we want."

Pete elbowed Scrub. "Go get that hamburger in the fridge. I bet he'll come inside when he gets a whiff of that."

"When you see a rattlesnake poised to strike, you do not wait until he has struck before you crush him," I said sternly, pressing on Bartleby's side. "Time to be off, boy."

"Hey, where do you think you're goin'?"

I began to walk backward. The ruffians followed. I sped up. So did they. I stumbled. What happened next can only be described by the legal term "temporary insanity," for I, Franklin Delano Donuthead, am a lifelong pacifist.

History has shown us, however, that Franklin Delano Roosevelt was not.

Being possessed of the spirit of our late, great thirty-second president is the only way to explain how the words *If you seek a pleasant peninsula, look around you* came out of my mouth.

I cannot accurately report what happened next, though I can reconstruct it from an eyewitness account. Bartleby jumped to attention. There was furious barking and gnashing of teeth; the ruffians beat it to the safety of the porch; I fell backward, cracking my head on the curb; and a passenger emerged from the car that was idling at the corner, watching us. She snagged her patterned nylons on the door panel and cursed before rushing to my aid as fast as her high-heeled pumps would allow.

Gloria, it turns out, is a bit of a fashion plate.

*Snap out of it, Franklin* were the first words I recognized. I was dreaming that we were on the phone together and Gloria had just related some particularly fascinating statistics with regard to longevity.

"Gloria?" I said, trying to make the picture before me come into focus.

"Yes?"

"Gloria?" I propped myself up on my elbows, taking in Gloria from head to toe. "This does come as a shock! I pictured you—"

"I'm black, Franklin. That's the common term. But I can pass for white on the phone."

"No, it's not that. I pictured you in sensible shoes, Gloria. You could turn an ankle in those things."

"Life is full of surprises, Franklin. I pictured you taking care of business. Now stand up. I just got this coat at Marshall Field's and I don't want to get it dirty.

"C'mon, boy." With one hand, she grabbed Bartleby's harness and, with the other, hauled me to my feet. When she was sure I could stand on my own, Gloria put her arm around me and pressed me close to her soft new coat. She smelled like the fresh flowers in Mr. Tranh's cooler.

"But how . . . how did you know where to find me?"

She opened the door and made a clicking sound with her lips. It was a sound that Bartleby recognized. He jumped into the car.

"Franklin, you're easier to track than a bleeding deer in snow, you know that? All I did was ask a few questions at the central bus depot and I was on my way."

"But you're supposed to be at an AURA meeting in Chicago."

"Those stat-rats need to spend more time in the real world, Franklin. I couldn't take it another day. So I cut out early, gassed up a rental, and loaded in the supplies." She reached over me and yanked on the glove compartment. Inside was a rawhide bone.

"Wait a minute. Nobody knew about the dog."

Gloria tossed the bone on the backseat, and the noises that followed were the sort that might have accompanied the untimely end of Scrub, Nick, and Pete.

"I guess it's time I let you in on a little secret, Franklin. I've got Bernie Lepner on speed dial."

"Bernie? You and Bernie Lepner . . ."

Gloria smiled. She wore lipstick! "Yes. I check on you, Franklin. . . ."

"Just like Sarah . . . ," I said, too overcome to say more.

"I don't have children of my own. You know that. And the fact is, you two grow on me. You surely do. Now let's go find Sarah."

CHAPTER EIGHTEEN

# Franklin the Brave-Hearted

Sarah Kervick's sense of direction left a little something to be desired. But I didn't mind. After all, I was cruising the run-down neighborhood in which she was staying in a brand-new Lincoln Continental with a state-of-the-art Global Positioning System. Gloria and I navigated in silence until we came to the corner of Lee and Algernon. There was the blue house, just as Sarah had said. She didn't mention that the screen door had no screens and that two of the windows had obviously been broken and were now covered in plastic. Even though it was only October, a blown-up Santa sat in the front yard, listing sideways at every gust of wind.

"Now, I want you to go up there and ask for Sarah," Gloria said.

"Me? By myself?"

"Sometimes, when poor folks see an adult dressed in business attire and they don't know her, they won't open up the door. I know this from experience, Franklin. It's either that or get all official with them. I prefer to try it this way first. Just ask to see Sarah. See if you can get her to come outside with you."

"All right."

I knocked on the front door. Nothing happened. I glanced back over my shoulder at Gloria. I knocked again.

A low, gravelly voice from the other side said: "Well, who is it?"

"It's, um, Franklin. Sarah's friend. I . . . can she come out and play?"

The door swung inward, and I came face to face with Mr. Kervick with breasts. Big ones. I had to lean back to avoid contact.

"You wanna what?"

"You must be . . . you must be . . . Aunt Zinny," I said, noting the dragon tattoo in the same location as Miss Mathews' mole. I willed myself not to blush. My brain needed all the help it could get.

"That'd be Zinny to you, 'less there's somethin' I don't know about."

"Franklin!" Sarah came charging down the stairs, only to be stopped by Zinny's arm.

"Hold up, girlie. Just where do you think you're going?"

Sarah narrowed her eyes and looked sideways at her aunt. "I told you about him. He's bringing my skate. . . . Is that it?" Sarah lost her composure when she saw the backpack slung over my shoulder. She grabbed for it, but Zinny knocked her arm away.

Sarah's hands balled into fists.

"Zinny is an interesting name," I ventured, hoping to avoid another disaster. "Would that be short for Zinnia? The flower?"

"It's Zenobia. Not that it's any of your business."

"Aah, yes. After the Greek goddess."

"What goddess?"

I had no idea, of course. The name did sound vaguely Greek, though, and my instincts told me that flattery was the best course of action here.

"Why, the goddess of compassion, of kindness . . . of beauty."

"You don't say."

"Mostly beauty, actually." I swallowed hard. "But kindness as well."

"Where'd you learn that?"

"I'm not sure. It might have been the library. Maybe the Internet . . . I could find out more if you like."

Zinny looked at the two of us like we were a couple of rusty pennies she had no use for. "Five minutes, on the stoop. Then *you* . . . back inside."

Sarah sat down with her back to the door. This did not seem to me to be the best tactical move. Plus, it was close to freezing and that cement stoop was cold! But we sat down anyway, and I put the backpack in her lap.

"Franklin, did I say you got promise? I knew you would come. I *knew* it!"

I think we both knew she was revising history. Waking up that morning, Sarah might have had a small bit of hope that I'd come. By afternoon, she'd worried it down to a shred. Who in their right mind would have believed I was capable of it? Not me, surely.

Sarah unwrapped the skate and kissed it!

"I been missin' this so bad. . . . Hey!" Sarah tugged out the teddy bear. She squished it between her fingers. Then she looked at me with that sad/angry/confused look that I now know signals the possibility of tears. But she didn't cry. Not right away.

She bit her bottom lip and pressed her eyes closed, pushing the teddy bear up against her face.

"You got feelings, Franklin. You really do. My mom gave me this."

We sat there for a minute in silence, the teddy bear cushioned between Sarah's head and her thighs.

"I'm afraid I couldn't wait, Franklin. I have got to meet this child."

Gloria stood in front of us. She really did look striking in her long camel-colored coat, her high heels, and—could it be?—the Vermilion Sunset color of her lips against her smooth, dark skin.

"It's Gloria," I whispered, and Sarah was off that stoop in a hot minute, throwing herself into Gloria's waiting arms as I sat there calculating our likelihood of future success with the game of life set at Fathers: 0, Mothers: 2.

"What's goin' on out here?" I jumped off the step and turned around. My principles of risk avoidance seemed to indicate that one should face Zenobia head-on.

Gloria reached into her pocket and pulled out her card.

"Gloria Nelots," she said. "National Safety Department."

"What's that got to do with me?" Zinny asked, letting the card flutter to the stoop. "Get back in the house, Sarah."

Sarah didn't move. Gloria cleared her throat and stepped forward. "I'm concerned about the welfare of this child, given the number of safety violations here. We've got broken glass, curb deterioration, no railing on the porch here—"

"Well, be my guest and get that slumlord over here to fix this mess. I ain't liable for a house I don't own, lady. And you'd best get off my sidewalk before I call the cops!"

Zinny stepped back inside and demanded: "Where's the cell?"

Sarah took advantage of the moment to pull us close to her.

"Offer to buy me," she whispered.

"Excuse me?"

"Rent me, whatever. Money talks to Aunt Zinny."

I blinked at Gloria. I was definitely out of my league here.

Gloria took hold of Sarah's arms and looked into her eyes. "You want to go back to Pelican View, is that it?"

Sarah bit her lip and nodded.

"Now, there's no need to call the police," Gloria said when Zinny returned, clutching her cell phone in her fist.

Gloria reached into her handbag and pulled out her wallet.

"What I'd like to do is give you a little something for your troubles."

"You tryin' to bribe me?" Zinny squinted at Gloria. I couldn't tell if the look meant she was offended or getting ready to deal.

"No, I respect you too much for that. But I do happen to have a number in Washington that advocates for fair housing. If you call this number . . ." Gloria extracted a pen and a little

notebook from a zippered pocket in her wallet. She also produced another card. ". . . and tell them what your beef with
your landlord is, my guess is he'll be over to fix it in no time
at all."

"I can't get him to come over here when my babies are
freezing," Zinny said, disgusted. "Now, you think a long-
distance call to Washington's gonna solve my problems?"

"No, I don't think. I know. Make sure to tell Mr. Rhetts that
Gloria Nelots is particularly interested in your case."

"So what do I have to do?"

"Just loan us Sarah. We'd like to take her back to Pelican
View for a few days. They miss her."

Zinny looked at the card in Gloria's hand. You could see
she was calculating.

"How long?"

"Not sure."

"She's been doin' the babysitting."

"Not long, then."

Zinny looked from one to the other of us, figuring. "So,
that's Franklin, huh?" she said to Sarah. "He don't look so
smart to me."

"He's pretty smart," Sarah said.

"And who's she?"

"Gloria. She's the one gave me the skates."

"So it's safe." Zinny shrugged and held out her hand for
the phone number. "Well, don't be gone long. And leave some
of them clothes for your cousin."

"Yes ma'am." Sarah darted past Zinny and up the stairs.
She reappeared in less than two minutes. Her skates, tied to-

gether, dangled over her shoulder. Her clothes were stuffed in a garbage bag.

Gloria picked her card up off the stoop and scribbled a phone number on the back. "This is Franklin's number. For the time being, this will be her contact. Her dad can call collect."

"I won't be seeing him till visiting hours, so I guess I had to make this decision." Zinny sighed, like making the decision to loan out Sarah Kervick was a powerful burden. I, too, was experiencing deep feeling. Gloria had memorized my phone number!

It was a homecoming to remember. Gloria called ahead and my mother was waiting, right along with Glynnis and Bernie, to welcome us back to Pelican View. Sarah had a foot out the door before the car stopped, causing Gloria to slam on the brakes and jostle my vertebrae in a most unhealthy manner. My mother held out her arms, like she had at the ice rink, like she had at the ball field, and took Sarah in with the kind of joy you'd think she could only feel for her own flesh and blood.

Bernie and Glynnis rushed up to me.

"Oh, Franklin, you were so brave," Glynnis said. "How did Bartleby do?" I got the impression that Glynnis might not resist a hug from yours truly, but I kept my hands at my sides. Really, who was this girl in front of me? If she would allow a dog to lick her mouth, she might be into all manner of unhealthy activities. What did I really know about Glynnis Powell, aside from her carefully groomed exterior?

"Well, Bartleby was not as vicious as you seemed to indicate, Glynnis. I was forced to use the state motto at one point in our journey, and he put up a good show, but he certainly didn't attack anyone."

"Oh, that's because the Michigan state motto is only his warning signal. It's the Nebraska state motto that means attack to kill. I didn't want you to be responsible for any physical violence, Franklin. I'm sure you aren't . . . well . . . you don't seem the type."

"What's the Nebraska state motto?" Bernie asked.

Glynnis looked from me to Bernie to Bartleby, who was now licking the remnants of a Thompson Treat from her palm.

"I better not say."

"Hey, you!" My mother grabbed me from behind in a bear hug. "When I get done bein' mad that you lied to me, I'm gonna kiss you!" She covered my hair and the top half of my face with some very wet kisses before whirling me around to look me in the eye.

"Franklin, what you did was generous and thoughtful and brave. I know you didn't tell me because Sarah made you promise—and that was very wrong. You never should have gone on your own. We'll have to deal with that later. But in another way, what you did was selfless. . . . It was *right*, Franklin. I mean it. I'm so proud that you're my son."

And she crushed me up against her with the same fierce concentration that she'd given Sarah. My mother has said some nice things to me. But she doesn't often tell me that she's proud.

"Will Sarah stay with us?"

"For a few days."

I smiled.

"What? What's funny? Is that okay?"

"Nothing. It's fine."

First Zero. Now Sarah Kervick. I do believe the authors of the "hygiene hypothesis" would approve.

"Well, I've got to catch an eight o'clock plane from Detroit this evening," Gloria said, "but I would dearly love to see one thing before I leave this town, and that is Sarah Kervick on ice."

My mother consulted her watch. "Paul's over there right now smoothing it out for the hockey league."

Bernie had to run home to get permission. Glynnis shook her head.

"He'll need to eat," she said, taking up Bartleby's harness. "Well . . . I guess I'll be seeing you, Franklin."

I couldn't believe how much easier it was to talk to Glynnis, now that I didn't hold her in such high esteem. She still had some fine qualities. I've said it before. No one's ears are cleaner than Glynnis Powell's.

"Glynnis, do you think . . . sometime . . . well, would you like to sit with us at lunch? I have some information to share with you from the American Council of Cheerleading Coaches and Advisors that I think you'll find very interesting."

Glynnis covered her mouth with the hand Bartleby had just slobbered all over. This was followed by the severe dilation of blood vessels in her face. She nodded yes.

"I almost forgot . . ." I reached into my jacket pocket for her kerchief. I had put it there this morning for good luck. Sadly, it was not as fresh as when I'd first laundered it. "I believe this is yours."

Glynnis reached out her hand. "I think it is. . . . Thank you, Franklin."

"It's nothing . . . all in the line of duty. Good-bye, Bartleby." I patted the hound. "Good-bye, Glynnis."

Words escaped her. She waved a hand in my direction and hurried off.

Sarah caught up with me in the parking lot of the Pelican View Ice and Fitness Center.

"You know what? I didn't think you were gonna make it today. I misunderestimated you, Franklin. I sure am glad I was wrong." She punched me in the shoulder.

"When I undertake a project, Miss Kervick, I always see it through to its conclusion."

At this, she laughed, throwing her head back and looking directly at the sun before walking—shoulder to shoulder— with me into the building.

I sat in the bleachers, wedged between Bernie and Gloria, watching Sarah Kervick move like a fish gliding through water. My mother was on the other side of Gloria, squeezing her thigh in anticipation.

"Here it comes," she said.

Sarah skated backward at a dangerous speed, preparing for her single lutz as Paul methodically cleaned the rink with his two-ton roller. Only Sarah Kervick would offer her back to a Zamboni.

"What you did was really amazing, Franklin," Bernie said.

"We should have a new name for you. It could be . . . Franklin the Brave-Hearted."

Franklin Delano Brave-Heart. I grinned. For I could easily see how, in Marvin Howerton's small brain, that would soon be translated to Franklin Delano Donut-heart.

Sarah landed her jump and transitioned into the spin. My mother and Gloria gave her a standing ovation.

"I saw your post on the memorial Web site," Gloria said after she'd sat back down. "To William. Thank you."

"You're most welcome, Go Go."

"Don't you call me that in public." Gloria kept her eyes on Sarah. But she was smiling.

And Sarah . . . Sarah was spinning. It seemed she could go on like that forever.

"I'm going to be honest," Gloria said. "I don't see how you managed that trip . . . the likelihood of you traveling by yourself to Grand River . . . well, those aren't betting odds."

"I don't know, either," I said. "I guess, for once, I wanted to be the hero."

## AUTHOR BIOGRAPHY

Sue Stauffacher's books for young readers include *Harry Sue* and *Donuthead*, the first book about Franklin and Sarah, which *Kirkus Reviews* called "touching, funny and gloriously human" in a starred review. To learn more about Sue, her books, and the making of *Donutheart*, visit her Web site at www.suestauffacher.com. Sue lives in Grand Rapids, Michigan, with her husband, Roger Gilles; her two sons, Max and Walter; her dog, Sophie; and her cat, Fig.